The Amish Twins

The Amish of Pride Book One

Emma Schwartz

Second Wind Publishing

Copyright © [2016] by [Emma Schwartz]

All rights reserved.

No portion of this book may be reproduced in any form without written permission from the publisher or author, except as permitted by U.S. copyright law.

Disclaimer

While this full-length Amish Romance with a joyful happily ever after is set against the backdrop of the fictional town of Pride, Ohio, a progressive Amish community, the characters, settings and names do not exist. There is no intended resemblance between Pride and any Amish or Mennonite community in the United States. Because this is a work of fiction, I've taken creative license with the setting, characters and activities, in order to provide a delightful experience. It is not possible to be accurate in all descriptions as all Amish communities differ, and any attempt to do so would destroy the entertainment value I'm providing to you, my faithful reader. Any inaccuracies portraying the Amish and Mennonite way of life are simply to provide you with a clean, inspirational reading experience. I hope you enjoy this novel about Pride and the wonderful Amish who call it home!

Prologue

The babies were crying again.

Wailing and draining her strength as if someone had slit her wrists and her life's blood was slowly draining.

Draining.

The pounding in her head increased, fueling the despondency that threatened to explode over her body in a torrential downpour of emotion.

She loved them; truly adored them with every breath in her body. But she wanted to be free. To run outside and feel the kiss of sun and breeze on her flushed face. To taste independence once more and be responsible only for herself and not a yoke of squalling infants. To wake up in the morning after a hard day's work in the garden without an alarm of mewling, starving, clinging ...

Without.

Alone.

Freedom. It whispered to her aloft on a cloud of desire. Then it screamed as if sprung from the fury of hell.

She slouched at the reins of her buggy, driving the rickety vehicle slowly. She couldn't afford a new one and this was her only means of transportation, so it had to last. Probably years longer.

The town of Pride, Ohio loomed before her, aptly named because 'pride indeed goeth before the fall.' And she'd fallen. Fallen so far down it was if she'd leapt from the moon and come crashing down to earth in a giant heap of bruised pride.

She had her sisters to help. But... her elder sibling had her own family with her own *kinner* and *mann* to take care of. And her younger sister, well, that wasn't to be thought about. Because that one had her own cross to bear. The bottom line became these *bopplis*. They were hers. Her mistake, so hers to raise on her own. Tears welled up in her eyes for even thinking it, even allowing the negativity to trail across the recesses of her mind. The *kinner* were a gift from *Gott*, just like all *bopplis*. Tough or not, she was their *mamm*. She had to figure out how to get through this.

But all the prayer in the world couldn't stop the feeling. The thoughts. The desire to stop feeling so old. And haggard.

And hopeless.

Up ahead loomed a structure... a home. One where the sound of a *boppli's* cries had once been welcome. At first glance, it looked like a temple lifted from the ancient times. The mist enveloped the two-story, white edifice and then soared above it like a shrine. Like a safe haven from times when things were more black and white even than her simple life. From times when women didn't have any control over their own destiny and couldn't make their own choices. Back when men weren't allowed to create *bopplis* and then leave without a backward glance, abandoning their family.

She slowed her horse to a walk as she approached as if seeing it for the very first time and relishing what it could offer her. What it could become.

She glanced back at the two lives behind her, strapped safely inside. The rhythmic clop of the horse's hooves on the pavement had finally lulled them to sleep. It was the first time she'd had any peace in the past twenty-four hours. They slumbered, their identical faces lush with dreams. They'd finally quieted but not so the noise in her head. And they'd start again. As soon as the buggy came to a complete stop, it would start. And it probably wouldn't finish until sometime tomorrow. Demands. Cries.

She sighed, looking at the *haus*, so still and solid. Would *Gott* be angry? Would He send down a bolt of lightning to strike her dead on the spot? If she kept the buggy moving, in a few minutes the structure would be behind her. Just like the rest of her life.

Her eyes widened as the idea sprang forth. Like a shoot of green beans in the springtime. And suddenly, there was a way. A way to regain her sanity.

She sat up straight in the cracked leather seat, *nee* longer hunched over her arms, *nee* longer hopeless.

She had to do something. And she'd do it right now.

Chapter 1

"Sarah! Sarah, you've got to come and see this. It's a blessing from *Gott*!"

Sarah Martin's heart throbbed in her throat as she stood in her living room. Those were exactly the kind of words a new *muder* wants to hear. Except, she wasn't a new *muder*.

Not anymore.

"I'll be right there." She mumbled in the direction of the wood burning stove a second before she hurried to see what had caused Suzanne's exclamation.

The high-pitched wailing had come from her best friend, Suzanne Fisher. She'd originally come over to have coffee but the overwhelmed Sarah had drafted her straight into duty, helping with some canning. Sarah tried to calm herself with the acceptance of Suzanne's assistance as she rushed to the rear of her home. Sarah lived with her Aunt Miriam, a widow who had taken pity on her and allowed her to reside with her in return for help around the *haus*.

But when she heard Miriam, who was well into her sixties and as sharp as the blade on the tiller, call out from near the front door in exasperation, her feet literally flew across the floor.

"Oh, Sarah. Are you almost here? You're just not going to believe this."

Sarah's stomach sunk down to her toes. Suzanne had a tendency to over-react but not Aunt Miriam. That meant she had trouble.

As far as she knew, all of the occupants of the home were accounted for. She and Suzanne had been in the kitchen leaning over the hot stove and Miriam had been sewing. Suzanne had offered to bring Miriam a cup of the hot brew. When her feet skidded to a halt in the hallway, Sarah found both women in a tizzy of excited movement.

"Isn't it the greatest miracle you've ever seen?" Suzanne exclaimed as she bent over a basket. Sarah couldn't understand why the two women were such aflutter over the basket of raspberries they had yet to turn into preserves. Then the strangest thing happened. Miriam leaned over and lifted the raspberries from the basket, bathed in swaddling. The fruit let out a high-pitched gurgle.

Sarah gasped and placed her hand over her mouth.

Miriam held up the wiggling infant for inspection, as if presenting it for baptism. "Well, aren't you the sweetest little *boppli*," she cooed.

Sarah knew this *boppli* didn't belong here. But her own precious *boppli*, Vernon, had been here. A joyous addition to this home. Her thoughts fluttered back to Vernon's precious face and then to her *mann* Levi. But then... the happy memory faded because they were both lost to her forever.

This was like some strange scene out of a fantasy where her *boppli* was returned to her. Alive. Miriam held the infant out to her but Sarah shook her head. She didn't want to hold it, so it would force her to feel something. It needed to go back home. Why was it even here to torture her?

"All we need is a clap of thunder and a flash of lightning to prove *Gott* is at work here," Miriam said as she brought both baskets in the *haus*. There were two of them? Twins? The sky darkened and the smell of rain permeated the air. "We need to bring them inside before they get rained upon."

"*Nee.*" Sarah's voice held upset and confusion but something else. Something even deeper.

Anguish.

"Really, Sarah," Miriam said, clucking her tongue, "they're little still. They need to come inside so we can decide what is to be done. Together."

Sarah stepped back as if the two infants were poisonous vipers, and Suzanne took one while Miriam took the other. She followed them aimlessly into the living room. The smell of the boiling raspberries overwhelmed the interior atmosphere, which was now also laced with talc. Sarah's morning had been so delightful until this point. Spending time with her best friend, Suzanne, chatting and canning. Miriam sewing in the living room. And now this. She felt like the walls of her beloved home were closing in on her.

So much for that content and satisfied feeling she held dear and had been eluding her ever since her treasured *boppli* and *mann* had been wrested from her. She still questioned the fairness of *Gott*. Of life.

"Where did they come from?" she asked.

Miriam glanced down and then started to rummage through the baskets. She came up empty handed. "Gracious, I really have *nee* idea."

Suzanne, her arms filled with *boppli*, stood closer to Sarah. Almost as if another life force had taken over her body, Sarah peeked over Suzanne's shoulder to gaze upon the *boppli's* angelic face. So perfect. Soulful brown eyes stared back at her as if the infant could see through to her deepest thoughts and feelings. Almost as if she knew her already.

"*Denke* to *Gott* they weren't outside in the elements for long," Miriam praised, swiping her index finger along the little boy's full cheek. "They don't even have a chill."

Suzanne bounced the little girl up and down and the *boppli's* eyes fluttered shut. "Miriam, what made you go outside when you did? Did you hear a knock?"

Miriam held up the little boy, dressed in blue and extricated his small, pudgy fingers from the white string of her *kapp*. "I heard horses trotting in the drive and I assumed it was Eli Troyer come to check on Sarah. But then, the sound went right back down the driveway again, so I ran toward to the door to see what Eli was doing. I didn't recognize the buggy or the horse. By the time I got on the porch, they were driving away. And my eyes. Well, you know they're not as keen as they used to be."

Sarah's mind raced. If Miriam had heard horses that meant someone had been here. Someone had abandoned their twin *bopplis* at her *haus*. On purpose. Who could have done such a thing? She didn't even know anyone in their tight-knit community with twins.

"After the buggy rounded the bend in the driveway, I couldn't see anything anymore and when I turned to go back inside, I saw these two precious angels in these wicker baskets, right beside the door. Oh, I wish Eli would come. Sarah, I think you should go and fetch him."

Sarah held up her hand. This wasn't the time for Miriam to start her matchmaking again. Eli was her friend. A very *gut* friend and since they were both widowed, they shared that common bond. "We need to find out who left their *kinner* here. I think I should fetch Bishop Beiler instead."

Miriam snorted. "What's that crabby old goat going to do with two sweet, precious little ones? He hasn't handled an infant in four decades."

Suzanne's *boppli* started fussing so she bounced her even harder, and Sarah feared she may spit up all over Suzanne's cotton dress. During one rather forceful bump, a piece of yellow legal paper drifted out of the child's blanket and fell to the floor. Sarah leaned forward and clutched the piece of paper to her breast.

"It's a note," she whispered. Not wanting to read it. Not wanting to know.

"What does it say, Sarah?" Miriam asked in a calm tone. As Sarah curled it open, Suzanne peered over Sarah's shoulder and narrowed her eyes as if trying to make out the words.

I know you can take care of Samuel and Emma better than I can.

I know what you've been through.

I trust you with my bopplis.

Gott is gut.

The lines were handwritten in script that Sarah didn't recognize. *Nee* name. *Nee* defining characteristics. How were they going to find the *mamm* of these *bopplis* on first names alone? Samuel and Emma. Common Amish names.

Hand to the back of her *boppli's* head, Miriam placed the infant against her shoulder, nodding thoughtfully as she glanced at the paper. "It must be someone we know. Since she said that she knows what you've been through, Sarah, it has to be."

"But we don't know any women in Pride who have had twins and all infants are accounted for," Sarah exclaimed, still not even close to understanding. "We have to give them back."

Miriam speared Sarah with a gaze. "Give them back to who, my niece? Should we abandon them a second time? Two wrongs don't make a right."

Sarah sighed. She didn't need this when she was just starting to live her life again, finding some enjoyment in her everyday activities. Trying to navigate the turbulent waters of this new situation, she dropped one hand on her aunt's slender shoulder.

"Perhaps," she suggested, "I should go fetch an elder before you have these *bopplis* staying here."

Chapter 2

Bishop Amos Beiler flipped closed the small notepad he'd been writing on while collecting his thoughts and pushed it away from him. Across the dining room table from the older man sat Sarah and Miriam. "And that's all either of you can tell me about the appearance of these twin *bopplis*?"

Sarah exchanged a look with her aunt. It was obvious what Miriam wanted Bishop Beiler to say and so Sarah sat there and held her breath.

"That's all the information we have, Bishop Beiler," Miriam confirmed. "Whoever left them isn't someone we know. At least personally."

The *bopplis* were still in the wicker baskets a few feet away, waving their tiny hands and kicking their feet. An occasional gurgle would float upon the air and each time that happened, Sarah felt an answering tug deep in her womb. Oh, how she wanted to pick one up and hold it close to her as she inhaled its clean and fresh *boppli* scent.

Because you want to pretend it is Vernon.

They were carbon copies of each other except one was male and the other female. They had thick, dark hair standing straight up and those soulful brown eyes that seemed to see everything. The first time she'd changed them and called them Samuel and Emma, she'd liked the sound of their names on her lips. Luckily, they were still far too young to be traumatized by these events. Sarah knew that Bishop Beiler was frustrated because nothing had come with the *bopplis* that might indicate their parentage.

"One of each," he said on a sigh, looking back and forth between them and tugging his spectacles as if he couldn't quite believe his eyesight. "Miriam, do you have any ideas? You've lived in this community almost as long as I have but you're more well-versed in matters of infants than I."

"Other than considering it an act of *Gott's* grace?" Miriam asked as she glanced at Sarah and a knowing look passed between her and the bishop. "No. I can't imagine who did this."

Cold gray eyes held Sarah captive. Before the words were even out of his mouth, she knew what they would be. And she'd fight him. *Jah*. She'd fight this request with every ounce of the devastated *mamm* inside of her. "I think you were this *muder's* particular choice, Sarah Martin. And we all know why."

She nodded out of respect, but she didn't care for the direction this conversation was headed. "We don't know it was a woman who abandoned these *bopplis*," she argued, grasping at straws. And light through her personal darkness. "For all we know, it could have been her *mann*, destroyed over her leaving him. Thinking he couldn't care for them properly."

"Possibly," he said. "But I think we all know that is highly unlikely."

Sarah glanced down at the chubby faces so peaceful in slumber. Much like her own precious son's had been. She used to sit by his cradle and rock him for hours, just to watch him sleep. Make sure he still breathed. Until one day, he didn't.

"I don't have any idea who did this."

And she didn't. If Sarah had known the troubled *muder* who had chosen to leave these perfect *kinner* on her doorstep, she'd have done everything within her limited power to reason with her before ever asking Bishop Beiler to come by and raise his mighty hand in judgement. The bishop was a *gut* man with integrity, but he had *nee* idea what to do in this situation. What was best for these *kinner*?

"What about Eli?" he asked.

Sarah's heart started galloping through her chest like a herd of wild horses. What did Eli have to do with this?

"What about him?" she countered. "He wasn't anywhere near my *haus* when this happened."

"Hmm ..." Bishop Beiler leaned back and tented his hands. "Maybe he should be near your *haus* more often."

The nerve. The audacity. Her own family hadn't even been in the ground a year, and yet everyone in the community seemed to be throwing her and Eli together like they didn't have minds of their own. Like they didn't have hearts.

Sarah looked at him sharply and pursed her lips together in a flat line. "No, Eli needs to stay at his own *haus* where he belongs."

Sarah saw her aunt shoot the bishop a warning gaze and crossed her arms over her chest for *gut* measure. She didn't need to be controlled like her every move was up for public scrutiny. Just because she'd been widowed didn't mean she couldn't take care of herself.

The bishop stood to leave and danced around the wicker baskets as he made his way around the table. "Well, I'll consult with my personal network and see what I can find out about the neighboring communities. He reached down to pat the little boy on the head. "In the meantime, I'm not in any position to care for these *bopplis*, being a widower myself."

He gave Miriam a pointed look, and her aunt didn't miss a beat. "We'll keep them until you find out who the parents are."

Caught off guard, Sarah hadn't really thought this through when Miriam had recommended fetching someone. She'd just wanted that person not to be Eli, lest he get any big ideas about the four of them becoming some kind of warped family unit. Of course, Bishop Beiler would want to leave the *bopplis* with her. But her feelings hadn't been considered and she didn't want the twins here.

Reluctantly, Sarah nodded. Where else could they go? She and Miriam were in a position to take care of them until a better arrangement could be made. Maybe Sarah would soften toward them in time. There wasn't any point in arguing further because her aunt had a stubborn streak as wide as a gorge and she'd already made up her mind, probably from the moment she'd found them on the front porch.

"All right, I guess we can keep them here," she conceded and Bishop Beiler's craggy old face broke out in a wide smile.

"Excellent," he said as he walked to the front door. "I'll see all of you at church this Sunday then?"

"Of course," Miriam answered as she stooped to pick up the fussy Samuel.

***

Sarah had been torn about the next step, knowing it had to be done, yet hesitating to do it. Not because of any doubts in her mind as to the competence of the man she was about to visit, but because of her own ability to remain calm during this face-to-face meeting.

With Eli.

But there wasn't any getting around it. Eli was the best furniture maker in all the county and he had cradles that were already made. She had nothing. So distraught over the loss of her son, she'd given away the cradle that her *mann* had lovingly made for him by hand. Sarah couldn't stand the sight of it. Now, her *haus* was empty of things that couldn't be hidden out of sight or stored in the barn. But she couldn't keep these *kinner* in wicker baskets. Not only was it unsafe. It was unsanitary. Eli would let her borrow a cradle large enough to fit them both, until something else could be done.

It seemed like ages ago that her childhood friend Eli had left their small community to follow his new *frau* home to hers. She had been a twin. A *twin*. Like Samuel and Emma. And she'd been reluctant to leave her identical twin sister. So they'd lost Eli. But then, cancer of the blood had taken Eli's *frau*, Mary, long before her time and he'd moved back to his family farm to restart his *dat's* furniture business. It had taken Eli very little time to reclaim his rightful place in their community upon his return. Now, it was like he'd never even left.

Sarah's footfalls hit the dirt of the path on the way to Eli's *haus* with soft thumps. She loved the feeling of the sun on her face and the wind in her ears. At first, she'd been reluctant to leave both *bopplis* with Miriam but Suzanne had stopped by to help out and so she'd agreed to go visit Eli and see about the large cradle.

She found him in his workshop, the hum of the diesel generator keeping him from hearing her approach. Sarah walked toward him and waved her hands until he glanced up at her. He brought the lathe to an immediate halt and took off his safety goggles. A beautiful mahogany table leg had been carved into an ornate design. Eli did such elegant work and Sarah admired it by running her fingers along the smooth wood.

"*Gut* morning, Sarah," Eli said with a smile. "What brings you by my place today? Did you want to take some air or is Miriam getting to you again?"

"Hi, Eli," Sarah said with a chuckle. "*Nee*. Miriam is just that. Miriam. Same as always. Something's happened, and I'm in need of your help."

Eli chewed on his lower lip and frowned. "It's not bad, is it?"

"*Nee*," she said. "I'm sorry, I didn't mean to scare you. At least it's not dangerous but I guess it is bad in a manner of speaking."

He reared back. "Now I'm really confused, Sarah. How can I help with this bad thing?"

After Sarah relayed the entire tale, he let out a low whistle. "Those poor, poor *bopplis*. I can't imagine who could have done such a thing. You're sure there aren't any identifying marks on them at all. Nothing?"

"Nothing," Sarah said as she walked around the lathe to stand closer to him and admire his design on the table. "This is just stunning, Eli. I hope to have a piece of your furniture someday."

"*Denke*," he said and ran his hand down the leg as well, stopping dangerously close to her own. She felt the heat radiate between them and a shiver went down her arm. "I'd love to make something special for you. But for now, I'll get that cradle ready for you to borrow and I'll drop it off at your *haus* later after I'm done working."

"I insist that you come for supper," Sarah invited him. "It's the least I can do to show my appreciation for what you're doing for the *bopplis*. That, and Miriam would tan my hide if I didn't offer to feed you. We'd just canned some of your favorite raspberry preserves when the *bopplis* were left on the porch and Miriam's made potato rolls. I'm pretty sure she's roasting a chicken in fresh herbs as we speak."

"If that's the case, how could I refuse? My own cooking is atrocious," Eli said with a grin and put his goggles back over his handsome face. "I better get this leg done, Sarah. I'll see you about six."

"*Wunderbarr*," she replied. "Miriam and I will be looking forward to it."

"And I'll be looking forward to meeting those *bopplis*."

Chapter 3

Eli crept his horse and buggy to a stop in front of Sarah and Miriam's *haus*, the heavy cradle on board. He tied his horse, Dancer, to the hitching post once he jumped down. He'd been surprised but delighted by Sarah's visit and that she'd finally asked for his help with something. He wished she'd do it more often. Actually, he was so pleased that he'd been whistling a happy tune the entire afternoon while finishing up the hand-scrolled table leg for Mrs. Schwartz's dining room set.

Sarah Martin had been avoiding him. And he didn't like it.

But her coming to him had been inevitable. She and Miriam were living in this big *haus* alone and he was an able-bodied widower who lived within walking distance. It was only right that he lend a hand to these female neighbors in need. But Eli hadn't expected seeing her alone in his woodshop to have had such a dramatic effect on him. Areas of his body still tingled from just the sight of her pretty face flushed rosy underneath her *kapp* and bonnet from her walk.

Sarah Martin was a beautiful woman.

Eli struggled to get the loaner cradle from his buggy and carry it to the front of the *haus*. He mounted the steps to the front porch where the *bopplis* had been left. Glancing around, he set the cradle down and inspected the area. He wanted to make absolutely sure the two women hadn't missed anything. He hunched down to check around the door for footprints, fingerprints, any sign of discoloration or something out of place. Nothing. Just like Sarah had said.

Eli knocked on the door and his heart thumped as he heard the footfalls of Sarah's dainty feet coming toward him. She flung the door open, her face alight with a smile of joy just for him. He inhaled a ragged breath and tried to calm his pulse.

"*Gut* evening, Sarah," he said.

She opened the door even wider and ushered him inside with a sweeping gesture. He bent over to pick up the cradle and set it inside the doorway.

Sarah gasped. "It's beautiful, Eli. *Denke* for allowing us to use it for these *bopplis*."

"Eli, is that you?" Miriam's tinkling voice called from the living room, followed by the upset squeal of a *boppli*. "Get your behind in here and help out an old lady."

Sarah sighed. "You better do as Miriam says, Eli. I'll see to the supper. I hope you like chicken, mashed potatoes and green beans."

"I do, indeed, Sarah," he said with a grin and then trotted off down the hallway toward the living room where he found Miriam holding a *boppli* on each hip.

"Here, take one," she said and held out the one dressed in blue. "This is Samuel. I know you and your dear *frau* weren't blessed with any *kinner* before she passed, but I have faith that you can do this. Just make sure his head is supported, like so."

Eli cradled the *boppli* and held him up to rest on his solid shoulder. The fact that he might drop him caused him to hold Samuel a little too tightly and the *boppli* started to fuss.

"I don't think I'm cut out for this, Miriam," Eli said with wide eyes.

"Loosen your grip, young man." Miriam frowned at him and proceeded to give a demonstration. "Samuel wants to feel secure, but not like you're trying to squeeze the breath from his body."

As he held Samuel and rocked him back and forth, he wondered how Sarah was taking having the *kinner* in her *haus* when her own *boppli* had died. Although word of the deaths had reached him, the details were vague and when Eli had returned to Pride, he was surprised to hear of the fishing accident that had taken both of their lives. Information tended to become skewed when it traveled via word of mouth from Ohio to so many states away.

It had been almost one year ago that Levi had taken little Vernon to the river to do some fishing. The *boppli* had tossed his favorite rattle in the rapids, and Levi had reached in to retrieve it while holding the ten-month-old. He'd slipped on some algae-covered rocks and he and the *boppli* had been swept away. The authorities assumed that Levi went under trying to save Vernon and their waterlogged bodies were found a few miles downriver about three days later.

"Eli." Sarah's soft voice jolted him back to the present and to the little *boppli* in his arms now. "I see you've met Samuel and Emma."

He never should have gone there with his memories. As he glanced at Sarah's beautiful face, still laced with tragedy, he wondered if she still missed Levi. Still loved him. If there was any space left in her heart for a second *mann*.

With effort, he tamped down the thoughts that he had *nee* right to think, pushing them away. He had *nee* business wondering about Levi Martin. *Nee* accountability other than being of service to his widow and helping her now that he'd found a way that he could. And perhaps, if she'd allow it, being a *gut* friend to Sarah. A better friend that he'd been when they were *kinner*.

"I'm really glad you were able to come by tonight, Eli," Miriam said. "Were you able to bring the cradle in your buggy?"

"*Jah*," he answered. "It just barely fit inside. I set it in the entryway, but I'll bring it to whatever room you want me to before I leave. It's much too heavy for you ladies since it's carved from solid oak."

Miriam glanced at Sarah and then back at Eli before she spoke. "I think it would be best if you carried it upstairs to my room."

Eli nodded as he bounced Samuel on his shoulder. The infant had quieted and seemed quite content to be in the large man's arms.

***

Sarah had thought once that she and Eli were friends. There might even have been a time when she'd hoped for more. When she'd wished that he would choose her. He'd been her first choice all those years ago, but he'd broken her teenage heart when he'd chosen another. Sarah had built a wall then, and Levi had scaled it. She'd tried to love him. But not as much as she'd loved Eli all those years ago.

Sarah raised her eyes and caught Eli's velvety brown ones with her own as he held Samuel in his strong arms. He and the *boppli* had matching eyes. For a fleeting moment, she wished they were married. That he was her *mann* and Samuel was her *boppli*. That this was their *haus* instead of Levi's Aunt Miriam's. She imagined the family she'd pictured as a girl. A loving family. He speared her with a heated glare. Almost like he could see deep into her soul and read her thoughts. She shook her head, clearing it of the cobwebs of memories. Clearing it of Eli, even though he stood not three feet from her with Aunt Miriam in the room.

"*Denke* for bringing the cradle," she said to break the oppressive silence. *Ach*. Was that all she could think of to say? She'd already expressed her gratitude. He must think her a fool. All she could do was remain thankful that he didn't know the depth of her feelings. She'd been *gut* at keeping her heart hidden all those years ago.

"It's my pleasure, really, Sarah," he said as he placed Samuel back in his makeshift bed of wicker. The *boppli* didn't make a sound but snuggled into the linens and sighed. "You're dealing with a lot right now, and I'm glad I could help out in this small way."

"Should we go and have supper since the *bopplis* are finally sleeping?" Sarah asked. "We can set their beds right by the dining room table in case they awaken and need feeding or changing."

Dinner was a lively affair. Anytime that Miriam got in front of a captive audience, especially male, she became inappropriately flirtatious for a widow of her age. After dessert, Eli insisted on carrying the heavy cradle up to Miriam's room and Miriam insisted she stay with the twins so that Sarah could show Eli the way. Even though she glared at her aunt in annoyance, Sarah stood at the top of the stairs watching Eli lift the cradle over his head as if it weighed only a few pounds. His muscles rippled underneath his shirt and she admired the way the fabric stretched over the expanse of his shoulders. All Sarah could do was stare at him until he stood on the landing and looked down the hallway and then at her.

"Which way to Miriam's room?" he asked.

She started and her head snapped up in embarrassment to be caught gaping at him instead of paying attention. As she walked down the hallway to the room, it was as if she could feel his hot breath grazing the back of her bare neck between her *kapp* and her plain blue dress.

"In here," she directed as she stood outside the door and gestured inside Miriam's room. Her aunt's bright yellow and blue quilt gave the room a cheery air and the twins would be very comfortable in here with the loving Aunt Miriam. She was so *gut* with *kinner*, having had five of her own. Miriam was happiest when her kids and grandkids came to visit, which was often. Everyone loved her.

After Eli set the cradle down gently underneath the large window, covered in plain draperies, he turned to Sarah. She stood still and watched him through hooded lids. Even though she knew she should leave the room, she remained rooted to the spot as if her feet were glued to the hardwood floors. Questions knocked around in her mind.

Why did you leave, Eli? Why did you choose another woman? Was she prettier than me? Was she a better frau than I would have been?

Sarah didn't vocalize any of her inquiries, and she never would. The past was the past and she needed to keep it buried where it belonged. So instead of turning around and leaving the room, Sarah stood her ground and expected him to read her mind.

He didn't speak.

"Miriam made that quilt," she said. It would seem she couldn't find her tongue tonight except to say something ignorant and boring.

"It's very cheerful." He smiled and glanced around. "The *bopplis* will be most comfortable in this room."

Sarah's pulse quickened as his face lit up with a trademark smile, and she felt it as surely as if she'd been hit in the stomach. Eli had always been so handsome. That hadn't changed. Her eyes held his for just a moment too long. Sarah tried to tell herself that she didn't feel anything for Eli anymore. All her love, her devotion, her grief, belonged to the family she'd lost. A torrent of emotions roiled in her stomach, threatening to bring back up the supper she'd only picked at.

"*Jah*," she mumbled and flew by him, finally breaking the spell of tension between them. Uncomfortable, emotionally charged unease that spoke much louder than any words could ever do.

Chapter 4

"Is the cradle situated underneath the window as I requested?" Miriam asked.

Eli chuckled to himself as he realized that the older woman had been standing outside the door the entire time, listening. Which meant the *bopplis* were downstairs alone. Miriam had made her intentions known all through the meal as she threw Sarah at him like some kind of widowed boomerang. She'd fly toward him but then she'd pull back and end up right where she'd started. Just like when they were kids. Sarah King, *nee* Martin, didn't want him.

And that fact broke his heart almost as deeply as it had the first time she'd rejected him. Although, judging from her cold and evasive reactions this evening, she didn't remember it. Didn't really remember *him*.

He sighed and ran a finger over the perspiration that laced his brow from the recent exertion. Miriam's eagerness hit him hard and Eli couldn't blame her really. She had to be bored living here with only Sarah and her family not visiting as often as they probably should. Life was hard for unmarried women in the community and two of them resided here alone without a *mann* to protect them. Miriam obviously thought it was too late for herself, but she wanted Sarah to be able to have a family again. To replace the one she'd lost.

Eli stared at Miriam. Her *mann* had passed away, too, so she should understand that family was irreplaceable. The three of them stood in silence in the narrow hallway, each lost in their own thoughts until he realized that Miriam was still waiting for a response from him.

"I did exactly as you asked me to," Eli responded and she nodded her pleasure at his answer. "Did you leave the *bopplis* alone downstairs, Miriam? I don't think that's really a *gut* idea."

Miriam snorted. "And what would you know of it, Eli? You've never been a *dat,* and I've raised five *kinner* to adulthood. Those *bopplis* are too young to get out of their baskets. The worse that could happen is that they wake up and start their wailing. Don't you think we'll hear them from up here?"

"All right," he said with a grin, amused at Miriam's feisty response. "I should return home then before it gets too dark outside."

The threesome walked down the stairs and Miriam stopped in the kitchen to get the *bopplis,* handing one to Sarah. The younger woman looked radiant and beautiful as she held Samuel in her arms and looked down into his angelic face.

"Poor little lamb," she whispered as she rocked him.

She was exactly right. Eli couldn't believe that someone had left their twins on Sarah's doorstep. What kind of *muder* did that? Child abandonment was something you expected to hear about in Cleveland and not in their rural community. Bemused, he turned to Sarah.

"Are you positive you have *nee* idea who could have done this?" he asked her.

"*Nee,*" she said as she shook her head and continued soothing the *boppli*. "Nobody we know had twins months ago. It's not the kind of thing a woman can hide in our community."

Eli nodded. Sarah was right of course and he felt stupid by asking the question. But somehow, questioning the horrific act out loud made some sense of it.

Eli knew the pain of a loveless marriage. And he'd struggled with the inappropriate feelings he'd carried ever since Mary had died. The feeling of freedom. Being released from the shackles of forced love that had bound him as surely as if they were manacles of steel.

Samuel let out a demanding cry and Sarah jumped. Eli knew that look. The petrified look like she didn't know what to do. What to say. She just stood there rocking him as he fussed.

"I'll stop by tomorrow and check on you both," Eli said as he turned to leave.

"You do that, Eli," Miriam said. "And plan on staying for supper. If you continue to force down your bad cooking, you'll waste away."

Eli said nothing, though the nod of his head became a little less animated, a little more forced. Miriam wasn't going to stop, and he wanted nothing more than to shout at her that she was barking up the wrong tree and her matchmaking would be better utilized on Sarah. There would never be any *bopplis* of his own because there would never be another *frau*. He'd never make another mistake like that, turning into his *vader*. Stretched out in bed beside the wrong woman every night, touching her. Lying to her.

He smiled as he walked toward the front door. Ever since he'd returned, he hadn't been able to escape the well-meaning community members who wanted to provide discourse on all the eligible women within three counties, providing an endless parade of feminine possibility. But he didn't want it. None of it. Because the only woman he'd ever wanted was standing behind him right now.

On the ride home, Eli could still smell the subtle and alluring fragrance of Sarah's soap. Lilacs. It reminded him of their childhood together. Running through the fields and standing beside her as they rolled old carriage wheels or picked dandelions. Memories danced across his mind, triggering thoughts of how much he'd missed her. It had felt *gut* to stand beside her again today inside her *haus*. Too *gut*. All the years had done was make Sarah even more beautiful to him. More desirable. More stirring. He'd hoped that time had taken its toll on her but it had not. Sarah tempted him, and he wanted to give in. But he wouldn't.

He hadn't left Pride in the first place to come sneaking back like a thief in the night. *Nee*. He'd left for a *gut* reason, and he'd come back for an even better one. He had extended family here and they'd welcomed him back with open arms. He'd married someone else and left for her happiness. Because he couldn't stay in Pride and see Sarah in love with another man. With Levi. The thought alone ripped his heart asunder.

Reaching his barn, he brought his horse to a stop and then jumped down from the buggy to unhitch the animal and put it up for the night. As he went through the motions, Sarah's face still flittered across his mind. He couldn't sweep her away. He'd just wanted to look at her holding the strange *boppli* and imagine what it would have been like to have her in his *haus*, holding their *boppli*. That thought made him ache as he threw hay to the horses like a man possessed.

***

The next evening, Eli stomped up the stairs to Sarah's *haus* in an attempt to shake the nerves from his wobbly knees. A light knock on the door was all it took, and he heard her footfalls coming to the door and the deadbolt slide open. Then, there she was. All grace, beauty and light. A punch to his stomach cavity.

"*Gut* evening, Sarah," he said. "I hope you're well and that you were able to get some sleep last night in spite of your new burdens."

She grinned and he felt it. Even more keenly than he had when she'd opened the door. The yearning. The wanting.

"*Jah*," she answered. "I did because Miriam is right on top of feeding and changing them as soon as they make the slightest murmur."

"*Gut, gut*," Eli said as he stepped into the hallway. Noting the silence. It just wasn't normal. "Where are they right now?"

"They're in the living room with Miriam," she said as she led the way. "They're sleeping. Probably a really *gut* time for you to peek in on them. Samuel has been very fussy today."

Eli admired the sway of her hips inside the confines of her plain, blue dress. What was the matter with him? It was like she'd already consumed him body and soul. He should have returned home for Levi's funeral. After all, they'd been friends for many years. But seeing her overcome with grief and love for the other man, well, that would have been more than Eli could take in light of his own pain. At that time, he'd already known that his *frau* was ill and that she wasn't going to improve. And the guilt... it consumed him still.

Eli owed Sarah an apology, if not an explanation. Before he knew what he was doing, he turned to her and placed a hand on her shoulder, staying her from going inside the living room where Miriam and the *bopplis* awaited them. He knew he shouldn't touch her. He didn't care. A jolt of electricity traveled from his fingers up his arm to his head and heart. Sarah twirled to face him and he let his hand fall to his side.

"I'm sorry I didn't return when you lost Levi and Vernon," he said, his tone stronger and surer than he felt.

She lifted a slender shoulder, letting his concern and his apology carelessly fall between them. "There wasn't anything you could do. *Nee* reason for you to travel all that way. It would have all been over by the time you got here. I'm sorry, too, you know. For your loss."

He sighed. Leave it to Sarah to take the focus off her own pain and try to be the balm for his. He had the oddest feeling that he'd failed her somehow, that she'd needed him and he hadn't been there. But that couldn't be true.

"*Denke*," he said, not wanting to elaborate. The memories belonged in the past, despite the disturbing thoughts he still had every morning after his nightmares told him he'd made a huge mistake. And then, when Mary had gotten ill, he'd experienced crippling guilt and shame. As if *Gott* were punishing him for even thinking he'd married the wrong woman.

Rousing herself, Sarah squared her shoulders. Her look was studied innocence, not giving anything away. Not revealing her true feelings. "Shall we check on the *bopplis*?"

He followed her inside the living room where Miriam sat in an oak rocking chair with Samuel on her shoulder. He'd been Sarah's friend once. But the look he'd seen on her face just now undid him, melting away all his noble intentions and making him want to just hold her in his arms until whatever it was that had bothered her had passed.

"*Gut* evening, Eli," Miriam said with a twinkle of merriment lighting her eyes. The older woman wouldn't be happy until he and Sarah were together in some capacity. And he couldn't blame her. He'd like nothing more. Unfortunately, he wasn't the half of the pair who would require convincing.

"Miriam," he answered. "I see you have Samuel all content this eve."

As he spoke, he walked over to gaze over Miriam's shoulder to where Samuel slept, his black, sooty eyelashes sweeping the tops of his chubby cheeks.

Sarah broke the spell between Eli and the *boppli*. "It's really dark in here, Miriam. I'm surprised Eli could even find his way. Why aren't more lamps ablaze?"

Miriam clucked her tongue as she balanced Samuel. "Really, Sarah? The *bopplis* are sleeping. Why on earth would I light more lamps? Do you want them screaming all through supper?"

Sarah turned red and Eli looked at her, puzzled. She'd been a *mamm* at one time. These emotional reactions were strange, pointing to Sarah's discomfort. He hoped he wasn't the cause of her behavior. Her words had him reaching for her hand, but he caught himself and let his own fall to his side, wanting to connect but not knowing how.

Miriam laid Samuel gently into the bassinet they'd borrowed from Suzanne and turned to Sarah. "Let's go into the dining room and have supper, shall we? Sarah has made a beautiful roasted rump of beef with vegetables and fresh corn bread. Of course, I have a fresh jar of those wild blueberry preserves I remember that you like so much, Eli."

His mouth watered thinking of Miriam's delicious preserves. He'd missed them. Most of all, he'd missed Sarah. Her kindness. Her beauty. Just *her*.

After they were seated, Miriam handed him a full plate and he took a bite of the succulent meat. Sarah had outdone herself. The beef and tender vegetables were seasoned to perfection. He was just about to compliment her on the meal when Miriam spoke first.

"So, Eli," she said, spearing a bite of carrot with her fork. "Have you brought your buggy into town to see the new bakery? An *Englischer* bought it from the Schwartz family and it's really gone downhill. The rolls are dry, and I almost had to spit one out of my mouth into the nearest trash receptacle."

Eli smiled when he saw Sarah roll her eyes and take a nibble of her cornbread. A crumb settled on her lush lower lip, and Eli had to blink away the fantasy of sweeping it away.

"*Nee*," he answered, giving his head a shake. Partly to answer and partly to remove the inappropriate thoughts of his hostess from his mind. "I've been into town but I haven't had a chance to stop at the bakery as of yet. Is there anything there that is still *gut*? I used to love the cinnamon rolls and I'd get one whenever I could."

"*Nee*, there really isn't," Miriam answered with a snort. "You'd best just come over here for freshly baked rolls and jam if your sweet tooth starts acting up."

Sarah seemed to be enthralled with moving her vegetables around on her plate. Her carrots became separated from her potatoes and beans. Each piece of food piled in a mound by color. "You're being very harsh, Aunt Miriam."

Miriam set down her fork and glared at Sarah. "That's just because you don't eat sweets. If you were as addicted as I am, you'd be feeling the loss as well."

Eli shook his head again. What was that *Englisch* line? *The more things change, the more they stay the same?* He'd been gone a long time but Miriam was exactly the same, even though so many things had come to pass for both him and Sarah.

"I think you would do well to lay off the rolls yourself," Sarah argued.

Chapter 5

"*Nee*, Sarah. You possess the most empathetic of natures. It is a miracle the *bopplis* were left here with you and Miriam."

Sarah would have believed Eli once, believed he meant what he said. Those flowery words settling in bone deep, flitting over her skin as if he'd caressed her. But he hadn't. Eli Troyer had never touched her romantically, even though she'd dreamed of that happening. She'd experienced so much pain and anguish that she'd married another man. Now, the guilt overtook her each and every night because she hadn't been the best *frau* she could have been. Or so Levi seemed to believe.

Eli sat next to her on the porch in a wicker rocker. He leaned back and then let his go into a swaying motion that caused his feet to lift into the air.

"Sarah," he said again, forced to repeat himself, jolting her out of her internal dialogue with ghosts from the past. "You have always shown every person and animal the utmost kindness. That hasn't changed."

She merely shrugged off his words, even though she welcomed them. But she'd not allow them to invade her heart now. That would wait until later when she was alone and allowed herself time to savor them. Once Eli knew who and what she was, he'd never view her in a kind light again. She'd killed her *mann* and her *boppli*. As surely as if she'd pushed them both into the river.

"*Denke*," she said, softly. Not knowing what else to say.

"Well, I better be going now," he said. "It looks like a nasty storm is brewing and I don't want to get caught in it. Thunder and lightning really scare Dancer. And the river still has that bad habit of overflowing at the worst possible times."

Sarah clamped her eyes shut against the terrifying mental image his words conjured. Eli had been looking to the sky but when he glanced sideways at her and saw her expression, he hissed in a ragged breath.

"Oh, Sarah," he apologized. "I didn't mean to bring that up. Please forgive my callousness."

She lifted one shoulder and let it drop. "There's nothing to forgive, Eli. You didn't mean anything by it. The river does have a tendency to flood this time of year and it's been that way for as long as I've lived here. All my life."

Sarah felt nervous, which surprised her. It couldn't be Eli making her feel this way, could it? He'd never upset her in the past. Maybe it was his innocent words that had gotten to her, burrowing under her skin in the worse way.

He looked at her for a long moment. "Well, I guess I should be going then."

The wind made its displeasure known, howling around them, flapping through the nearby trees and lifting leaves and debris to skitter across the earth's surface. Self-preservation leapt up within her heart, bringing another shrug to her shoulders and two words to her lips. "All right."

Ach, why couldn't she be more charming and articulate like she'd been in the past? Well, because the darkness had touched her soul and it enveloped her body still, creating a shroud of black netting.

Eli flinched and Sarah felt the guilt again. So many negative emotions continued to overtake her small stature, she didn't know when one ended and another began. He stood and ran a finger through his thick hair before putting his hat on his head. A strong gust of wind reached underneath the brim and threatened to carry it away. Eli put a hand up to steady it and scrunched up his nose as the first raindrop hit him.

Before Sarah knew what was happening, he reached his free hand out to clasp hers. It was warm. So warm. Hot, really. Everywhere they touched, her skin burned. She felt branded but told herself the innocent caress had been extended in friendship. Empathy. Support. But then, she was a lousy liar and she always had been. The touch meant so much more. Another raindrop fell and landed on his upper lip and all Sarah wanted to do was kiss him. To suck the drop away. Taste him.

Just a single rash action. Just this once.

But rash actions had stolen her very life away, so she stood still and stared at the hand that caused the rioting sensations to course through her body like a runaway freight train. Her breath evaporated a second before she felt the pressure of his thumb swirl a circle on the tender part of her palm.

Sarah's mind drifted back.

Back.

To the time when they were *kinner*. She'd known the exact moment that she'd made her choice and decided that she'd wanted Eli. They'd been picking turnips in his *mamm's* garden. Sarah had been on her knees in the dirt with the spade, dirt soiling her stockings. Eli had stood a few feet away, catching fireflies in a jar for her. When he'd finally caught one, they'd made a wish, pretending the light was a shooting star falling to earth.

Gott, I wish that Eli will be my mann someday. Please, Gott. I know this should be our path.

Her head began to swim wildly. Either from her memories or from his scalding touch. Or both. The force of the feelings caused by his light strokes rushed through her. Gentle. But rough at the same time. A whisper of a caress that felt like the weight of a thousand boulders bearing down on her heart and soul.

The impact wasn't lost on Sarah. Everything had changed. He'd changed the trajectory of the journey and there was *nee* going back because now she'd felt it. She'd felt what it would be like to belong to him.

Lightning flashed a few hundred yards from where they stood.

Connected.

Their own special brand of chemical electricity. The thunder followed. A boom that caused Sarah to jump and Eli to hold her hand even tighter. This calm before the storm only magnified the sound of her pounding heart. A pulse throbbed at the base of her neck.

She'd been waiting years for this one touch.

There were some things that the passing of years, with their seductive powers, enhanced, playing an impish trick that made you believe that something was actually better than you thought it ever could be. But time had played *nee* such follies with Sarah. If anything, time had muted the impact, leaving the sweetness but deleting the power.

It all rushed back to Sarah now. All the feelings that she had ever harbored for this man. All the feelings she'd kept hidden every day of her life. Even though she stared at his hand touching hers, she didn't pull away. She couldn't.

There was absolutely *nee* doubt lingering in her mind.

Touching Eli had been worth the wait.

Chapter 6

It wasn't enough.

Like a single, teasing drop of water to a thirsty man, the touch only made him yearn for more. Crave more. Eli struggled not to weaken further than he already had, but it was like sinking into quicksand. The more he mentally thrashed, the deeper he sank.

Ach, he was a man and not a boy. A man who had already been married once. Built a life for himself and prepared for a family. He wasn't supposed to be acting with a boy's careless disregard for danger in this way. Lightning flashed again, a bright reminder of nature's fury. *Gott* wasn't happy that he'd succumbed to his inappropriate yearning for Sarah Martin and was making *His* displeasure known.

Sarah represented danger personified, because he'd realized in just this short amount of time that yearning for a life with her made him forget all the guilt and shame he should be feeling. She made him forget all his noble ideals and effectively reduced him to a walking blob of needs and desires.

He. Should. Not. Feel.

But somehow, though he wanted only to wrap his arms around her, to kiss her senseless and see if she'd soften underneath him, he managed to pull himself away from the center of the vortex that had almost succeeded in sucking him in. The devil's vortex.

More shaken than he'd thought possible, he took a deep breath before he trusted himself to look at her. *Ach*, she looked even more beautiful, flushed rose from the electricity of their touch. Something had passed between them. She knew it. He knew it. And yet, it was wrong.

It might even be a sin.

"I'm sorry, Sarah," he whispered. "I should not have done that."

She shook her head. "*Nee*, you shouldn't have."

Why, when she was agreeing with him, did her words feel as if they were all sharpened daggers, poking him with their verbal blades? Why did the vapid look in her eyes make him feel even guiltier? Shame over his dead *frau* washed over him. Shame over Sarah.

Eli hurried to make any atonement that he could. "It's just that..."

"Just what?" she asked, the two words dripping with icicles.

Talking would only make things worse, Eli realized. He'd never had the gift of eloquence, especially not at soothing women's ruffled feathers. Especially, when he knew he was wrong. Eli only knew the truth and that couldn't be uttered. Not now. Probably not ever.

I want you, Sarah Martin. More than I've ever wanted anything in my entire life. I wanted you then and I want you now.

He wished she'd show him a sign. Anything to keep his hope alive and burning within the depths of his chest. Then again, he hoped she wouldn't, because her doing so would make the fact that they were so close and yet so far apart unbearable.

Turning from her frosty stare, he did the only thing he could do. He retreated.

***

"Is Eli gone, Sarah?" Miriam's voice jolted her head up. *Ach*, she hoped that her aunt wouldn't start with a string of questions. Questions she didn't want to answer.

Miriam stepped out onto the porch and looked to the violent sky. "I was hoping he'd stay and wait out the storm. I don't like the thought of him getting struck by lightning on the way home. How on earth would I explain that?"

Sarah stood perfectly still, in direct contrast to the turmoil roiling through her stomach cavity. What had she just allowed to happen? What was wrong with her? Levi had only been cold in the ground for twelve months and here she was touching someone else. Welcoming the caress of someone else. She wished a fresh bolt of lightning would shoot from the darkened sky and electrocute her. It was what she deserved. For being so brazen. So loose.

"Are the *bopplis* still asleep?" That was a safe question. "I'm surprised the thunder didn't wake them."

"*Jah*," Miriam said, looming over her. "Is everything all right, Sarah? You look flushed. Are you well?"

"I'm well," she said, calmly. "Just a little distraught over the weather."

Her aunt's eyes narrowed. "It's just a summer storm. It will pass."

It would pass. If only that were true with everything else.

Sarah nodded and stood to follow Miriam back into the *haus*. She walked to the kitchen and peered at the sleeping Samuel and Emma. Miriam had been right and they still slumbered peacefully. She sank into a wooden dining chair.

"I may be old, Sarah Martin, but I know what's going on here," Miriam said. "I'm not senile."

Sarah's head snapped to attention. "I'm not following you, Miriam."

The grin that took over her aunt's face was like a cat that licked the cream. "You know." She winked instead of answering specifically. "I always did think the two of you belonged together. I never understood why he married another woman and left."

Oh, Miriam. If only you knew the truth.

Sarah frowned, unwilling to reveal anything of consequence. "Oh, I don't know about that, Miriam," she finally said, surprised by the strength in her voice. Because she didn't believe a word of what she'd just uttered.

"You can say what you want, Sarah Martin," Miriam argued as she pulled a rattle from Samuel's bassinet. "I see the way he looks at you. The way you *try* not to look at him."

Sarah didn't need this right now. She clasped the rattle in her hand and gave it a little shake. Not enough to wake the *bopplis* but enough to make her feel better imagining it was Miriam's shoulder. Biting off a choice turn of phrase, she let it ticker tape across her brain but remained silent.

"There's nothing there." A warning note permeated her voice.

Because there was something there. In fact, everything was there.

Everything.

"Have it your way." Miriam sniffed. "But I know better. I know the truth and I know that Eli is part of *Gott's* path for you. If he wasn't, *Gott* never would have led him back home at exactly this time."

Sarah leaned down to run a finger across Samuel's soft cheeks. It amazed her how much he resembled Vernon, her own *boppli*. The heart that remained broken skipped a beat at the thought of losing Vernon. And Levi. All of a sudden, tears clouded her vision and she wanted nothing more than to flee to the safety of her bedroom and cry in peace over what she'd lost. But even more so, over what she desperately wanted but could never have.

"You're not getting any younger, Sarah," Miriam said with more kindness than she'd laid down with the previous statement.

"I realize that, Miriam," Sarah said, snatching her hand back and placing it in her lap.

Sarah stood, anxious to get away from her aunt and the one-track conversation because she already felt derailed. "I'm only twenty-two."

"That's over a quarter century younger than I am," Miriam said. "It's too young to be giving up on life. On your own family."

She was being too edgy, Sarah thought to herself. Miriam cared for her and Eli and was trying to help, thinking she knew best. Maybe she did. And under other circumstances, things might have turned out differently.

"You do understand that another woman will take him from you," Miriam said, her lips pressed into a thin line. "He's a fine man and would make any young lady a worthy *mann*. The catch of Pride. And then you'll be sorry you remained so stubborn."

Miriam's remark caused the blood to pound in Sarah's temples. Flashes of Eli with another woman sickened her. Telling herself that Miriam was making these inflammatory statements on purpose didn't help the nausea churning in her stomach. "Who?"

A pleased, knowing look highlighted the older woman's expression. "You don't like that thought, do you?"

Ach, she didn't like what she was revealing because doing so was only going to add fuel to Miriam's already blazing fire of meddling. Did Eli already have his eye on someone in their community? Is that why she'd had to seek *him* out? Why he hadn't come to their *haus* to call? Their community was small and usually items of interest such as the new man courting a local woman would reach her ears relatively quickly. Suzanne would be over immediately to relay any new gossip.

Miriam patted her forearm. "It's alright, Sarah. I don't know of anyone right now. I was just speaking in generalities. So you don't make a rash decision. One you'll regret."

Chapter 7

By morning, the twins had given new meaning to the word demanding. Sarah rolled over in her bed and placed the down pillow over her ringing ears. Miriam's room was far too close to hers now, even though it was the farthest down the hall.

She'd had *nee* idea after one *boppli* that two would be so much more difficult to manage. They seemed to be on completely different schedules with different wants and needs. They didn't sleep at the same time, they slept in tandem. *Nee* sooner was little Samuel asleep then Emma started wailing, her high-pitched squeals pealing through the entire *haus*. Their cries seemed to have woven a web right around Sarah's heart. Now, she couldn't imagine what she'd do if silence reigned.

Sadly, Sarah and Miriam were both lacking in sleep and their moods reflected it. Normally, they weren't so short with each other, having such a wealth of mutual respect that they got along famously.

Bopplis or no, Sarah doubted if she could have slept very well anyway after experiencing Eli's touch. Every time there was a blessed second of silence for her to close her eyes, she fantasized about him. Reliving the feelings he'd ignited in her body. Feelings she'd never experienced even when she'd been married. But then, it had always felt that way between her and Eli with a yearning that couldn't be extinguished.

She washed in her basin and then teetered down to the kitchen for breakfast and coffee. She needed that cup of hot brew today more than ever. As Sarah had expected, every woman within walking distance wanted to speculate about the *bopplis* left on the doorstep, so the knocks on the door started soon after she and Miriam had finished eating. The dishes weren't even completed.

She served so many cups of coffee and potato rolls to her friends and their *mamms* that she felt like her head was going to explode. The same variations of questions were asked over and over again. Sarah felt like an automaton, going through the motions and nodding and speaking at exactly the right places but saying nothing of consequence. Her temper was getting progressively frayed and the well-meaning women preyed on her last nerve. That, she knew, was more a result of her sleeplessness than any ill will toward them and their curiosity.

Once the last guest finally left their *haus*, it was past noon. Samuel and Emma had been poked, prodded and squeezed until they'd finally fallen into a fitful sleep. One of Samuel's tiny fists fluttered around his lips. She closed the door on Suzanne and leaned against the door jamb, a limp rag doll of overextended emotion. It took a supreme effort not to sag against it and slide to the floor.

It was a moment before she realized she wasn't alone. Miriam stood behind her with Emma in her arms. Of course, it would be too much to ask that they'd both stay asleep at the same time.

"You don't look well, Sarah," Miriam commented with a cluck of her tongue. "Did you get any rest at all last eve?"

"Some," Sarah lied.

The truth is that every single time I shut my eyes visions of Eli dance through my head.

"Well, the dark circles under your eyes say differently."

Sarah was quickly realizing how futile it was to argue with the woman, so silence was her best option. They stood staring at each other for strained moments when a knock at the door broke the tension. Sarah squeezed her eyes shut. Not another visitor. Not now.

The effect of Miriam's obsidian glare faded and Sarah stiffened. She took a quick mental inventory of everyone who'd stopped by and what other woman could possibly be left to entertain today. She couldn't think of one. That meant that whoever was at the door didn't have any friendly reason to be there. Bishop Beiler?

Probably the local authorities or social services. Those *Englischers* rarely frequented their tight-knit community but the thought had crossed Sarah's mind that these were extenuating circumstances that might cause an unsolicited visit.

"I'll get it," Miriam announced. "You should go sit down, girl. Before you fall down."

Sarah's arm snaked out, stopping her. "Please, make them go away. I don't think I can take one more question."

Miriam nodded. When the door swung wide and Sarah peeked out of her half-open lids, she saw the bishop standing there and not anymore abandoned *bopplis*. A wave a relief floated over her trembling body.

Bishop Beiler stepped over the threshold at Miriam's gesture, his tall frame filling the foyer. Just like Eli had done the day before. One glance at the man's face caused hope to surge through her body.

"Did you find the *bopplis mamm* already?" she asked, her voice raised with expectation. "I admit, I thought it would take longer."

The bishop cleared his throat and motioned to someone standing on the porch behind him. The white of a *kapp* appeared, then her shoes, then a plain blue dress with a protruding belly. Sarah tried to stifle a gasp but didn't succeed.

"I didn't find the *bopplis mamm*, Sarah," he said. "But I did find *her*. She says she's a cousin of yours." As he stepped out of the way, Sarah saw the identity of the mystery woman for the very first time and her heart sank to her shoes. *Ach*, no. It couldn't be. And yet… it was.

Caught between being stunned and overjoyed, Sarah found herself struck speechless. Between the lack of sleep and now this, she didn't think she could push any coherent words past her parched throat. But what she lacked in words, she made up for in gestures. She threw her arms around the woman, taking care not to squeeze her *boppli* bump too tightly.

Releasing her, Sarah stepped back and drew her very pregnant cousin into the *haus*. "Katie, *ach*, look at you." Her eyes swept over Katie's ripened form. "When did this happen? I didn't even know you were expecting."

Instinctively, Katie placed her palm over her growing belly. "Seven months ago."

Sarah gasped. How could this news not have reached her and Miriam? Katie only lived a few counties over. Sarah stared at the door and Bishop Beiler because someone was missing. Where was Katie's *mann*, Jacob?

Sarah couldn't believe Miriam remained silent but the older woman simply stood and stared at the entire scene as if she were watching the events play out and she wasn't participating in them.

Puzzled, Sarah gave Katie a searching look. "Where's—?"

"I'm sorry." Katie's eyes welled with tears. "He's not here."

A lonely droplet escaped her cousin's eyelid and trailed a rivulet down her flushed cheek. Now was obviously not the time to press. Sympathy poured through Sarah. Maybe this was simply a little spat fueled by raging pregnancy hormones and would soon blow over. This would be Katie's first *boppli,* and Sarah could remember the out-of-control feelings, like emotion might overtake you at any second. "Is there anything I can get you, Katie? A glass of water or milk?"

Katie smiled at Sarah and swiped the tear away with the pad of her finger. "I need a place to stay."

"It's that final?" Sarah asked, a small sigh escaping her lips.

Katie nodded. "*Jah*." Tomorrow was another day and she'd probably be able to wrest further details after the sun rose in the morning.

Sarah knew what it felt like to have your future evaporate right before your very eyes. To see it slip away and have it be your fault. To experience the residual guilt and shame until it threatened to overtake your very soul. In order to cover the awkwardness Sarah knew that Katie felt in this very moment, she changed the subject. "Why didn't you just knock and come on in?"

Katie's smile was contrite. "I came with Bishop Beiler in his buggy. I found a ride to town, but I didn't feel I should walk the whole way here."

Behind her, Miriam cleared her throat rather loudly, about to say something.

"Where are my manners? Miriam Martin, this is my cousin, Katie Eicher. And this, Katie," Sarah said, still a little flustered by Katie's strange appearance out of the blue, "is Bishop Beiler."

Something akin to tolerant amusement flittered across the bishop's face. "We've met. On the way here. In my buggy."

Sarah flushed beet red. "Right, I apologize." She flashed a contrite look in the elder's direction before turning to Katie again. "I guess you just caught me off guard with the unexpectedness of your visit and your condition."

"I remembered what you always said about Pride, Sarah," Katie said, averting eye contact. "I wanted to come to a place where I'd be welcome. So I can think while I wait for my *boppli* to arrive."

"Well, then," Miriam said. "You've certainly come to the right place. The place where you can get *lots* of practice."

Confusion shone on Katie's face. Since Samuel and Emma hadn't made a sound, she remained blissfully unaware of the twins. Miriam took the younger woman's hand in hers, effectively welcoming her to her *haus* and taking her under her controlling wing. The only *gut* thing about this day was Katie coming to take the focus off of Eli and who his future *frau* should be.

"*Denke*, Mrs. Martin, it's so *gut* of you to welcome me in this way."

Miriam waved away the formality with a shrug. "Everyone calls me Aunt Miriam and I think I have the perfect place for you. It's the bedroom right next door to mine."

Bishop Beiler nodded his head. "*Gut* thing I brought Katie here straight away."

"She's always welcome here since she's family." Sarah nodded. She knew Katie would be eager to see her bedroom and the rest of the *haus,* but it would be rude to leave Bishop Beiler standing in the foyer after his hospitality and protection of the pregnant Katie. "Bishop, I feel that some coffee and fresh potato rolls with jam are in order. Would you follow me to the dining room and I'll prepare some refreshment before you return to town?"

"I'd like that," he said as he followed Sarah. "Miriam makes the best jam in the county."

"Funny, that's exactly what Eli said yesterday," Miriam mumbled and took Katie's hand again to propel her to the dining room chair.

"Coffee and rolls it is then," Sarah said as she slipped a slender arm around Katie's shoulders and ushered her into her seat. The pregnant woman collapsed with a large plop. It appeared the journey had exhausted her, and Sarah felt bad about the long conversation in the foyer where she'd had to remain on her swollen feet.

The adults engaged in some getting reacquainted conversation while they enjoyed their refreshment. After about an hour, Bishop Beiler stood at the door to take his leave. Just as he reached for the doorknob, a loud knock rang out. Miriam rolled her eyes.

Bishop Beiler turned to face the women. "Are you expecting anyone else today?"

Sarah sighed. "I don't believe there's anyone else in Pride who hasn't already been here."

Bishop Beiler pulled the door open for Miriam. The sound of a man's deep laugh registered at exactly the same time as Eli's excuse tumbled from his full lips. "Sarah, I thought I'd drop by and check on the *bopplis*..."

His eyes ran from the bishop to Katie and back, confusion lighting his features. "I'm sorry, I didn't mean to interrupt anything." Of course, since Eli had just returned, he'd have *nee* way of knowing that Katie was from three counties away.

Bishop Beiler nodded a greeting. "You're not. I just dropped off Sarah's cousin, Katie, and I'm returning home. *Gut* day, ladies. Eli." And with a tip of his hat, he was off to his buggy.

"Well, I'll just show Katie her room then," Miriam announced. "Sarah and Eli, can you keep an eye on Samuel and Emma?"

Aiming a triumphant smile at Eli that Sarah knew couldn't be misinterpreted, Miriam left the couple standing in the foyer.

Feeling awkward after the tension of the previous evening and the distress of the day, Sarah cleared her throat. "I just got done serving Bishop Beiler and Katie some refreshments. Can I get you anything, Eli? The *bopplis* are in their bassinets in the dining room."

"*Nee*," he said. "I just had lunch a little bit ago. I got to working in the wood shop and I lost track of the time."

Why did he look so refreshed? Like he'd gotten plenty of sleep and wasn't bothered by their interaction of the previous evening? Because he was a man, that's why. His emotions didn't affect him like hers did. Sarah would do well to remember it. She straightened her shoulders and sucked in a deep breath, steeling herself for the conversation to come. If he were a gentleman, he wouldn't mention anything.

Eli leaned over the bassinet and put his large palm on Samuel's chest. The *boppli's* light breathing caused Eli's hand to lift. The same hand that had touched her. Sarah clamped her eyes shut against the image because it brought the fresh memories back in a rush of emotion that she didn't want to feel. A veritable river of feeling that threatened to overwhelm her if the dam didn't hold.

Chapter 8

"Is this the first time they've both been sleeping this afternoon?" Eli asked.

"*Jah*," Sarah said, sliding into the chair opposite where he stood, hoping he'd follow suit, so he wasn't towering over her.

"It's most tragic when people die before their time."

Eli stated the obvious, the one thing that couldn't be denied because it was what had brought him back to Pride.

"Huh?" Sarah's head snapped up and she looked confused. "What brought that on?"

Eli slid into the seat next to her, feeling like after last night, it was time to have the conversation. He didn't want to hide anything from Sarah. Never again. "Mary passed away," he said, softly. "And I feel guilty about it."

The silence hung heavy in the air. Eli held his breath, hoping she wouldn't shame or reject him.

"I feel guilty about Levi's death, too."

He couldn't help it. He reached out and put his palm over her closed fist. Radiating his support through to her. Levi Martin had been madly in love with Sarah. So much in love that Eli had pushed his own feelings aside and left Pride after his *gut* friend, Levi, had confessed how deeply his adoration for the beautiful young woman ran. Then, Eli had run. Fled Pride and everyone and everything he knew, chasing down the first woman who'd smiled at him because he knew he couldn't stay. It would have torn him asunder to stay and watch Sarah fall in love with Levi Martin and build a future with him. His friend and sometimes rival. He wasn't strong enough for that.

Sarah stared at their hands touching, but she didn't move hers away. Sitting there together, allowing the strength to flow between them while they verbalized their shared weakness, felt right. As sure as breath and life.

He wanted to do more. To wrap his arms around her and stroke her hair. Take the pain away. "You didn't need to leave, Eli. Why did you leave?"

The next words wouldn't come. So much for the honesty he'd wanted to lead with when he'd started this conversation. Now wasn't the time to admit his feelings and admit they'd never died.

"I had to."

The simple admission was all he could muster. Sarah stared at him, her eyes revealing nothing. Why didn't she say something? Anything? Then again, it was selfish of him to expect her to assuage his guilt with lighthearted words of forgiveness.

She pressed her lips into a thin line and then a spark kindled in the depths of her eyes. They blazed as she opened her mouth. He wasn't going to get the words that would serve as a salve on his soul. Not today. "I needed you to stay. You were the only other person who knew what Levi was dealing with. I could have used a friend and a confidante. I had to hold it all inside. My burden, Eli. When it should have been all of ours."

With a sigh, he wrested his hand from hers and ran it through his hair. The frustration settled in bone deep. Because Sarah was correct and he really had nothing to say that would ever make this situation right. He might never be able to bridge the gap between them.

"I thought I was doing what was best for you by leaving." The words sounded trite even to his own ears.

She stared at him with open animosity. He'd never seen a look quite like the one she now wore. Certainly not directed at him. "That's ridiculous. Why are you lying to me, Eli? You had to know how lonely I'd feel. Lonely in my own *haus* even with two other people!"

He flinched as her words peppered his body like sharp rocks. If the floor would open up and swallow him whole, he'd jump in and allow the darkness to envelop him. He'd failed her, and he'd never forgive himself for his actions.

Sarah continued to take great heaving breaths and he just stared at the rise and fall of her chest underneath her chaste blue dress. He didn't like her so angry. *Ach*, he hated her so angry at *him*. His stomach roiled and nausea bubbled up the back of his throat.

"I know." There really wasn't any use arguing or trying to defend himself. Nothing *gut* could come of it and doing so would simply widen the emotional abyss between them.

"Do you realize that I didn't sleep last night? Because of you and what remains between us? Not to mention the fact that some random *muder* dropped off twin *bopplis* on my doorstep with nary a backward glance? Do you have any idea how stressful that situation is, Eli? Sometimes, I just feel like screaming."

All of a sudden, a grin tugged the edges of his mouth upward. The image of her screaming, all heaving torso and limbs, floated across his imagination.

"Why don't you?"

She gasped and her lush mouth fell open. "That's ridiculous. There are *bopplis* here. And my cousin, Katie, just arrived to stay."

He stood and held out his hand. "Let's go outside then. Where you can scream in peace and *nee* one will care except the wild critters that hear you and scamper away in fright."

"I can't just run outside like a toddler and throw myself down in a temper tantrum. I am a grown woman, Eli." Her voice trailed off in a huff as she ran out of words and steam. Because his idea really wasn't that bad.

"How about if I let you hit me?" he offered instead, a twinkle in his eye to match his smirk.

She simply stared at him as if he'd suddenly sprouted two heads. He reached out his right arm and gave her unobstructed access. "Go ahead, Sarah Martin. Wallop me. I can take it."

She snatched her hand back and held it to her chest as she shook her head. "*Nee*."

"Well, I thought I'd make the offer. It would probably make me feel better to have you hit me. As *gut* as it would make you feel to do it."

Now, she clutched both hands to her chest and began to wring them. "I'm sorry."

"For what?" She'd done nothing to be sorry for.

"I snapped at you because I'm exhausted. I had *nee* right to question you leaving when I'd already married someone else. It was wrong of me, Eli."

"I'm sorry, too, Sarah," he said softly. "This conversation was best saved for another, less stressful, time."

Sickness took up residence in his stomach because he'd really failed Levi, too. Who knows if his leaving had really even accomplished what he'd intended. Sarah was sitting here before him saying she felt the same guilt that riddled him with its pervasive cloak every time he was alone. Their marriage must not have been as satisfying as Levi had wanted. Because Sarah might have been in love with another man.

Me.

"I know you think you did what was best by running off, Eli. I know that you believe that. But it's not true. At least that's not my truth."

Eli leaned back in his chair and crossed his arms. Sarah was merely pointing out what he already knew. "Maybe I was afraid that if I stayed I'd lose both of you. We'd never have been able to keep the secret from him indefinitely. The truth always comes out, and he'd never have forgiven me. Then, he'd turn that resentment on you. What kind of perfect family would that have been?"

Eli thought of Sarah's own parents. Of how her *mamm* had told him how steadfast and loving her *dat* had always been. That's the way it should be between a married couple. His own parents and then him and his *frau* Mary... well, it had been as *gut* as it *could* be under the circumstances. But not like what Sarah's parents had enjoyed before they were so tragically killed. Sarah didn't deserve further misfortune.

"We never should have done what we thought was right, since it turned out so wrong. Hindsight has made the path clear and we took the wrong one. We should have prayed harder and asked *Gott* for a solid sign. The best decision wasn't made because it was made out of guilt. Levi should never have married me." Sarah stood and visibly shook. Tears escaped her lids and rolled down her flushed face. "If he'd married someone else, he'd still be alive!"

Eli stood, too, and grabbed her by her upper arms with a slight shake. "You can't say that, Sarah. You can't blame yourself. Levi and Vernon were killed in an accident. You had nothing to do with it."

Her face turned a pasty white. Eli gently guided her back into the chair. "You're wrong, Eli. I killed them both as surely as if I'd followed them to the river and pushed them in."

Eli scrunched his face up in confusion. What on earth was she talking about? She was taking her guilt over losing her family to an extreme. He briefly wondered if she were having some kind of mental breakdown due to the stress of having the strange *bopplis* in the *haus*, making her safe haven awash with a torrent of unpleasant memories.

"I need you to explain it to me then."

"We had words the day he took Vernon to the river," she whispered. Color still hadn't returned to her face. Eli's heart ached at her wretched expression. Sarah wasn't seeing him though. She'd retreated into her solitary world of pain.

"Words?"

Her vacant stare gazed at a vase on the sideboard. Still seeing nothing. "He knew, Eli. He knew why you left. I didn't say anything. I didn't have to. Somehow, he already knew."

Eli's mind raced. Searching. Replaying every single conversation he'd had with Levi over all the years he'd known him. He couldn't think of anything he'd ever said that would have led Levi to the conclusion that Sarah had married him out of pity.

This wasn't the time to dwell on that because Sarah needed him. Eli wondered what Levi had said or done to her to make her so devastated by the memory. He opened his mouth to ask her when a shrill cry pierced the air and all thoughts of grilling her further faded away. Knowing more about Levi would have to wait for another time.

He squeezed his eyes shut against the din. The wailing became louder with each passing second until Samuel's head appeared in the doorway, held by Miriam. The older woman looked back and forth between Eli and Sarah. She must have noticed the tension as well as Sarah's expression because she clucked her tongue as she bounced Samuel up and down to soothe him.

"Let me take him," Sarah said and held out her hands to take Samuel. He quieted immediately.

"You have the touch with him, Sarah." Miriam walked over and slid into the chair beside Eli. Katie wasn't far behind her with Emma. The younger woman balanced the *boppli* on her own pregnant belly.

Eli looked at Sarah holding Samuel and a pang of regret overtook him. She looked so *gut* holding him. Natural. Like he belonged in her arms. He looked at the face of the gurgling angel and longed to whisk Sarah away to his *haus* on a beam of light and become a ready-made family. The one he'd always longed for but only with her.

"It makes you wonder why someone would just want to toss them away. Like trash." His voice pierced the air, directed at Sarah but she hadn't even acknowledged him. Or anyone else in the room for that matter. Her gaze remained affixed to Samuel's face.

If Sarah had belonged to him, there was *nee* way he'd ever let her go. Her and any *kinner* they ever were blessed with.

"I think their *mamm* knew exactly what she was doing when she left them here," Miriam said. "She knew they'd be taken care of with Sarah."

Sarah's eyes finally lifted from the *boppli* and searched his. "She may have known exactly what she was doing. But they can't stay here. If they do, I'll ruin their lives just like I did my own when Levi and Vernon died."

***

A few days later, the exhausted women sat around the same dining room table. Katie's hands rested gently on her abdomen and the twins rested in their bassinet making gurgling noises. Katie insisted on doing more than her fair share of chores and child care in return for them letting her stay at the *haus*. Sarah was just happy that Miriam's laser focus had been taken off of her and Eli.

A knock at the door caused Sarah's head to snap up. She hadn't seen Eli since the day of their deep conversation and although her body yearned to be close to him, her mind wasn't ready for any further discourse on the subject. She just felt numb.

Miriam stood and opened the door. "Bishop Beiler. I'm so happy to see you. Come in and take some refreshment."

After the bishop was seated at the table with lemonade, biscuits and jam, the conversation turned to the reason for his visit. "I just wanted you ladies to know that your initial thoughts about the *mamm* of these *bopplis* being from farther afield appears to be correct. I was having coffee at the bakery yesterday," he said as he ran a fingertip around the rim of his glass, "and Joshua Miller told me he remembers seeing a random woman in a buggy the same day the *bopplis* were left here."

"And he recognized nothing about the vehicle? The horse? Nothing about her? *Nee* distinguishing characteristics at all?" Sarah fired the questions at Bishop Beiler as if doing so would cause the answers to materialize out of thin air.

"*Nee*, he didn't notice anything out of the ordinary except the woman herself. She drove more slowly than was safe and seemed bemused. I had to take this information to the authorities. Sheriff Kent is looking into it. He said that you'd be amazed at what you can find out even with the tiniest of clues. Judging from the time the *bopplis* were left here, he can narrow it down to communities within that distance from ours."

Miriam nodded. "Seems it's all in the right hands. *Gott* will provide guidance for us all, even Sheriff Kent."

"The sheriff also did something else," Bishop Beiler said after a bite of his biscuit. He brushed the crumbs from his lap. "He asked the county judge for a court order granting Sarah temporary custody of the twins while the investigation is ongoing."

Sarah stared at the legal-sized, gold envelope being held out as if it had fangs and could strike. It seemed so final. Like they may never leave. She took the paperwork and held it. Not wanting to open it. Not needing to.

Chapter 9

Sarah wasn't sure exactly what drew her to it, only that she had a sudden, irresistible urge to visit the old oak tree that stood on the edge of the Martin property. As she stared up at the expanse of gnarled branches ripe with leaves, drinking in the tree's energy, she imagined Eli cutting it down and making a dining set out of it. She shuddered. Picturing Eli's muscles bunching underneath his shirt while he wielded the ax made it difficult for her to draw breath.

She had *nee* idea why she felt tears stinging her eyes. So inane. Maybe she was suffering from summer allergies. Sniffing, she blinked the offensive water back from the recesses of her eyes.

Maybe it was Eli's mere existence that had drawn her here to the hundred-year-old hardwood, or maybe it was just an overwhelming urge to revisit a time when there was *nee* death, *nee* painful feelings and life still held the promise of endless, joyful surprise. Of simplicity and family. Whatever it was, she couldn't help herself. She had to come here. If for nothing else than for a moment's peace to hear herself think.

It wasn't that she didn't love having the extra people in the *haus*, especially her cousin Katie, who was proving invaluable in helping with the *bopplis*. And Katie loved the practice. She loved them. Most of all, she missed her *family*, as much as she tried to deny it to Sarah and Miriam.

So after supper was over and everything spotless, Sarah had appealed to Miriam for a few moments to herself to take the air. The warm breeze kissed her face and she slid down the rough bark of the tree to land in a relaxed heap at the base of the trunk. Tucking her legs underneath her, she rested her forehead on her knees.

Miriam had placed a shawl into her waiting hands and practically shoved her out the door. She had look well pleased that Sarah wanted to get out of the *haus* and commune with nature and so told her to take her time. All would remain well at home.

She wondered who had planted the majestic tree a century ago or if an errant acorn had fallen from another mighty oak of the past and thus, new life emerged. New life from the cold, dark ground. Ashes to ashes and dust to dust. Sarah stared at the sprouts of lush grass, heard the birds singing around her and marveled at the work of *Gott* everywhere she glanced.

She imagined Levi's *mamm* looking out over the trees and staring with love upon her only son as he played in the field across from the forest line. Without the burden of his chores. Running free and full of life, hope and promise. And she'd... she'd taken that away from him. Except for Aunt Miriam, Levi's family blamed Sarah and she'd gladly taken that on like a cloak of guilt.

Sarah imagined Eli playing with Levi here. Nostalgia overtook her as she drifted back to savor every memory of the three of them together as *kinner*. Friends. Hearts and lives entwined. She supposed that explained her uncommon connection to Eli now. Not because she truly loved him or wanted him but because his presence made her feel closer to Levi and Vernon.

Who was she kidding? She had feelings for Eli. Then and now.

Levi had envied Eli his talent with crafting wood and his passion to carve every piece into a thing of beauty that came directly from his heart. Levi had farmed the land just like the male generations before him, just going through the motions. He'd never shared with Sarah if there was anything he'd prefer to be doing. That was just Levi's way. He'd started out a kind and gentle man. A man of *Gott*. Until the day that he wasn't. She'd do well to remember *Gott's* path. Her current behavior was not only inappropriate, it was dramatic and went against everything she believed in.

A soft smile curved her mouth as she lifted her face to the cool breeze again. She'd known better, even then. But the lure of Eli had called to her and it wasn't until that fateful day when Levi declared himself that she'd even considered another choice. She'd known that the Eli who existed just beneath the carefully crafted façade was someone entirely different. Someone she didn't really know anymore. It was that person who she'd spent hours talking to under the warm afternoon sun. That person who she felt had become her very best friend. And he had been – then.

Ach, she'd told people that she'd been Levi's soul mate, but wasn't that what a woman was supposed to say about the man she was marrying? But Levi had never been as close to her as Eli had been. Eli still owned her soul. All parts, light and dark. Sarah wondered if Eli truly knew what he held in the palm of his hand. The ability to crush her if that's what he wanted. But he wouldn't, because he wasn't that kind of a man.

Which was why Eli had left town so abruptly and married another woman. One she didn't even know. That's the part that hurt most of all. He'd taken everything away from her because he'd taken himself away, even her ability to catch a glimpse of him at church. Everything had gone dismal for her that day.

After a while, she'd felt completely adrift, betrayed by the very values she'd clung to so tightly.

But she hadn't come here to ponder her lost ideals, or even Eli for that matter. She'd come to indulge in a welcome break. To try, for a moment, to recapture a feeling. The feeling she'd lost. Of youth, excitement and hope. A time when she'd found gratitude in everything and everyone. She wanted that sensation back, if only for a few stolen moments.

A sliver of moon appeared in the darkening sky, turning the blue a shade of navy. Sarah knew she should be heading back but her legs felt leaden and she indulged in just a few more minutes. The *bopplis* would be fine with Miriam and Katie, even though Sheriff Kent's paper made them her responsibility.

Sarah stared through the tree line. If she concentrated, she could just make out the roofline of Eli's *haus*. Located about a half-mile away, the property loomed in the distance like a scary scene that she didn't want to see but couldn't look away from. When she'd been a lot younger, she'd actually thought of Eli as a savior.

Rising to her knees, she looked off in the distance but a rustle of grass caught her attention. She stilled. A boot appeared in her line of vision. Than a sculpted leg, then a whole body. The one that caused her heart to start galloping as if it were striving for the finish line in a buggy race.

Eli.

As if in an emotion-induced haze, she placed a hand over the racing organ. "What are you doing here?"

He seemed as stunned to see her as she was to see him. Pleasure spilled through her as he grinned at her question. "I just felt the need to enjoy the warm air and commune with nature. Can I sit?"

She gestured to her impromptu grass blanket with a hand. "Of course."

"I used to love this tree when I was a boy," he said, leaning back against it and clasping his hands behind his head. The movement made his upper body even more pronounced and Sarah moved away. The closeness and heat was too much for her, and she had to evade the emotions he caused within her rioting body.

"I loved it, too," she admitted, twirling a blade of grass between her fingers.

She reached down and rifled through the bed of green, searching in vain for a four-leaf clover. That was *gut* luck in the *Englisch* world. She supposed she might never know his reasons for handing her over to Levi on a silver platter. Or his reasons for leaving her. Either way, he'd still left and deep inside, she resented him for it. And she had *nee* right. *Nee* right at all to feel those emotions.

"Finding anything?" he asked, his soft words slicing through the tense silence.

"What?" Her head snapped up and she glanced at him to notice the twinkle lighting his eyes. "*Nee*, I'm searching for a four-leaf clover."

"I think the *Englisch* have a song about that. I heard one singing it one time when I visited the bakery."

"I've never heard it." Sarah looked away again and resumed her mission of rifling through the grass.

"I'm sorry I made you uncomfortable the other day."

"You didn't make me uncomfortable," she lied.

"Sarah," he said as he sat up and came closer. Too close. "You're leaning so far away from me that the only thing keeping you from fleeing is the fact that you're sitting down. You're stiff as a board. Why are you so afraid? I'm not going to hurt you."

You already did and you have nee idea how much.

Chapter 10

"I'm not afraid," she whispered.

"Maybe not afraid," he answered. "I think you don't want to be around me anymore."

"*Nee*, I want to be around you too much."

He ached to touch her. Reassure her that everything would be all right. But her rigid back facing him instead of her beautiful face warned him away from it. A declaration was hot on his tongue, but he remained silent. He had to go slow with her as much as that frustrated him.

Their bodies hovered inches away from each other, but it might have been the distance of a gorge. He pushed the temptation from his mind. Instead, he watched her turn her head and catch her lower lip in between her teeth. "I should get back to the *bopplis*. Miriam and Katie shouldn't be alone with them this long."

"Stay."

The one word escaped before he could stop it. She turned back around and stared off into the distance. He had more faith in the future than she did. That was all right, because he had enough faith for the both of them. *Gott's* path was clear. *He* wouldn't have led Eli back here if it wasn't.

Since her back was turned, he allowed himself the pleasure of letting his eyes sweep over her from the white of her *kapp* to her sensible leather shoes. He tried his best to seem detached when every muscle was tense with a yearning to touch her. If he succeeded in his indifference, he was a better actor than he ever thought he could be.

Eli hissed in a breath, not sure if his struggle was due to the breezy evening air pushing the leaves on the ground or from her presence so close to him. It couldn't possibly be because the love of his life sat here, alone with him, mere inches away after so many years apart.

"It's beautiful out here," he said. "So peaceful. Do you remember spending hours outside in this area when we were *kinner*?"

"*Jah*," she said, still staring off into the distance. "It would be hard to forget. We laughed, ran and played. Talked about our hopes and dreams for the future. For our families. Remember how time moved so slowly we thought the future would never come? Now, sometimes... I wish it hadn't. That we could go back. Make things turn out differently."

Eli's heart ached at the words. "By the time we turned fourteen and were done with school, the future was already there, reaching out its hand for us to hold. The future came, just not as expected."

He remembered his *Rumschpringe*, making plans to leave home and experience the outside world. Escape the shame that chased him and forced him to run away from Sarah and Levi. That was when he'd still believed he could elude his love for her and that it was possible to distance himself from what haunted him.

Sarah shrugged. She'd never been as eager as he or Levi to forge ahead into the unknown. Her sense of wanderlust had never really materialized. Sarah had always been content to stay home and nest. For the first time, he wondered if that was because she didn't want things to change. And his leaving... well, that had changed everything.

"I don't know," he answered. "There are times when going back to the past, before things got so complicated, would have been welcome."

"*Jah*," she replied. "The past. It was so much simpler."

He thought she was referring to Levi's sudden death. "I can understand that." Eli had *nee* idea how to convey his sympathy to her. Probably like she had *nee* idea how to convey hers to him. The news of the tragedy, losing a young *mann* and a *boppli*, had deeply affected him as well. "I know it had to be devastating, losing them both on the same day."

Sarah pressed her lips together into a thin line of pain. What was the sense of her agreeing with him? Saying anything? Nothing she could say would ease her loss or his.

About to get up, he stopped. Sarah turned and looked into his eyes for the first time since he'd sat down beside her.

"What?" she asked.

"Nothing." But his look urged her on. He'd never been *gut* at hiding anything from her. And he wanted to steal just a moment longer and stay here, absorbing the memories. Absorbing her. "An admission then. I'm really enjoying being alone with you. Getting to know you again."

She smiled. A lighting of her face that twinkled like the first stars starting to litter the sky like tiny diamonds. It always surprised him, this feeling that would overtake him at the slightest softening of Sarah toward him. It was all part of his desire to be better now than he'd been then. When she'd needed him and he'd failed her.

Looking back with an adult's eyes, an adult who had withstood the most horrible of tragedies, he saw that it was Sarah more than Levi who had shared the thoughts he had been willing to impart to her. About his hopes for the future. What he wanted from his life and what he believed *Gott's* path to be for him. Sarah, who had kept his counsel and his secrets.

Always Sarah.

She had married Levi Martin. Because he'd told her to. Not knowing at the time that the decision would be the devastating mistake that destroyed his life.

"It wasn't the laughter that made you the one I can't forget, Eli," she said.

"Then what?"

Sarah closed her eyes for a second and he held his breath. Waiting. What would she reveal? When she opened them again, he realized that the journey had been unnecessary. His yearning for her hadn't really changed. It still made his heart race just at the sight of her.

"There was something in your eyes, something about you. Like *Gott* had shown his light down from the heavens and pointed the way for us. Except... we didn't follow the path. We chose to go a different direction and now we're being punished. What we wanted was dangled out in front of us. We didn't take it and now it's been snatched away. It won't be offered to us again, Eli."

She was wrong. The path was lit again and this time, they'd take it. He'd lead and she'd follow. It couldn't be any other way. Eli shook his head, although she'd turned around again. Probably not wanting to face him and acknowledge anything he was saying. Her heart was closed to him for now. She'd chosen to lock it and throw away the key. But he'd find it. And he'd open it.

***

The romantic in Sarah had faded away like the sun dipping below the horizon. "I don't think you ever truly understood the effect you had on me back then."

She glanced back over her shoulder to see him waving away her words. He was letting their past bond color his judgment.

"You and Levi were probably my closest friends. I haven't had a real friend since then."

Closest, maybe, she allowed. But what about his *frau*? "Mary wasn't a friend?"

"*Jah*," he said with conviction. "Mary was a lovely woman. She didn't deserve to be less than. To not benefit from my best effort."

Sarah nodded. She understood because it was the same guilt and shame she struggled with every night when the darkness caged her.

Sarah remained silent. There was something about this moment, the two of them sitting in the dusk with the moon highlighting Eli's face, which twisted her insides into a tangle, wanting things she could never have. He couldn't suspect the depth of feelings she had for him. Had always had.

"She must have been such a *gut* woman for you to marry her," she whispered, staring at his full lips. He looked as if he wanted to kiss her.

Don't try and kiss me, Eli.

Oh please, kiss me.

But instead, he drew back and stood. He was right. It was time to go, before one of them gave in to the temptations ravaging their bodies. Sarah popped up too quickly, lost her balance and fell, her arms floundering. Pin wheeling. Sarah struggled to get her bearings. A tiny gasp escaped her throat as she crashed toward the ground.

The next moment, Eli's arms closed around her, pulling her to him.

Saving her.

Chapter 11

The air left Sarah's lungs as if it had been sucked out by some old-fashioned blacksmith's bellows. But it was the proximity of the man and not the fall itself that had done it.

Grasping his arms to steady herself, Sarah could have sworn she felt Eli's heart beating just above hers. The pounding just as rapid as her own.

"As the closest furniture craftsman in the area, I recommend you don't go falling at my feet like a log." A hint of a smile moved across his lips. "Or at least not until your feet are firmly underneath you," Eli said, loosening his arms and holding her away from him.

Sarah felt the loss immediately.

She didn't want to extricate her limbs from his. Not yet. She knew she should, but she just couldn't seem to back away. Cocking her head, she looked up. Those eyes, they'd been her undoing so long ago and they still were. Eli stared into her own as if he saw everything. The things she revealed as well as the things she kept hidden. Sarah gazed upon the face she knew as well as her own, memorizing every contour, every plane. As if it wasn't already branded in her mind and in her heart.

"*Denke*, Eli."

He released her. "I won't always be here to catch you."

I know that.

A vision of Eli, holding out his arms to catch her, flittered across her consciousness. It took a second for her to find her tongue again. "*Jah*, you won't."

"But we can work something out," he said with a grin. "I won't leave you alone to falter."

Work something out? *Ach*, how desperately she wanted to work something out with him. "Do you promise?"

The smirk softened the features of his face, making him seem almost boyish. The boy she'd always known, instead of a man in his mid-twenties. "*Nee* promises, remember? If you don't ever make any, then you can't break them."

He winced and she knew he referred to his exit from Pride. But he'd made those promises. Just not with words. His eyes had told her one thing and then his actions had betrayed him. But whether he'd said them aloud or not, he'd always been there for her. Until the day that he wasn't.

Sarah struggled against a wave of bittersweet feelings.

And lost.

Before she could dig in again, she found herself being swept away. Not being able to stem the tide, she rode the wave of emotion. Going with her instincts.

Rising up on her toes so that her face was level with his, Sarah placed her palms on Eli's bare forearms, feeling the rippling muscle underneath. Reveling in his hard strength. She couldn't have articulated what possessed her to do it. To be so forward. In the past, he'd touched *her* and she'd allowed it. This time, she was the aggressor. He didn't move away. Just stared at her delicate fingers grasping him as if she owned him.

She needed to feel the heat of his skin underneath her own. Feel that wild, intoxicated feeling of doing something wrong. That emotion surging through her, taking her prisoner as it went on an all-too-fleeting ride. The emotion she'd only felt with this man.

Eli's face scrunched up into a grimace and he appeared to be struggling. He brought his arms up to rest on her slender shoulders and she allowed her hands to travel with the motion, not wanting to break contact. She wanted to discover all his secrets, old and new, right here under the dusky blanket of twilight.

All her life, things had come easily to her – except the one thing she wanted most of all. And that thing was standing before her. Touching her. But Sarah didn't want to be a wanton harlot, ignoring *Gott's* wishes and plan for her life. *Nee*. And that meant she couldn't let the rioting emotions and heat of her body get in the way of doing the right thing. But that right thing was so difficult when Eli was close to her. Wanting her, too. When she could feel him, warm and plaint and willing to sin. When she could sense his hunger and it matched her own.

Sarah could feel Eli withdrawing and he finally let his hands drop to his sides. She squeezed her eyes shut against the rejection, even though she knew it was for the best. He'd left her again. As surely as he had the first time, even though he was only a few inches away.

Shaken, she drew back. A woman had her pride, even if there wasn't much of it left. She looked down at the grass beneath her now steady feet. "I'm sorry, I guess my hands must be as clumsy as my feet."

Passing his palm along her cheek, he raised her head until she was forced to meet his gaze. "Don't ever be sorry, Sarah. Not with me. I should be the one apologizing again."

Didn't he have any idea how much that stung? It took effort to keep her voice steady, to keep her emotions from spiraling out of control. "For what?"

"For touching you. Before and now."

Why?

Her mind screamed the question over and over. Why did it seem so wrong for him to have feelings for her? For them to want a connection with each other? To go back and replace what they'd both lost and build a future? She interpreted it the only way she knew how.

"Is this only because of some loyalty you feel you owe Levi and your guilt over his death? Your leaving Pride?" The questions probably weren't fair. Pain and rejection propelled her forward to prod him in a sore spot.

When Eli didn't respond, she took his silence as agreement and her blood started to boil in her veins. Anger at the unfairness of the burden of the secret they both carried. "Maybe if you'd stayed in Pride, you wouldn't feel so badly about what's happened."

"I knew Levi, Sarah. I'm well aware of what happened and how it affected him. I'm not sure what you're saying?"

"Nothing." What was the sense of dragging up the things that went on between a *mann* and *frau*? Of the icy delusion that was the hallmark of their marriage? Maybe if he knew, Eli would even put the blame on her for what had happened. And maybe part of it was her cross to bear.

How many nights had she lain awake, thinking that if only she'd been a better *frau*, he'd never have slapped her that fateful day? There were far too many times to count where he'd raised his voice in anger. Levi had turned into his *vader* because it was the only life he knew. The same *dat* who had beaten him to a pulp the day he'd declared his love for her. Sarah shuddered as she remembered holding his battered body. His face bloodied and his wrist broken.

Eli had been there, too. He knew why she'd married Levi and they'd moved into the *grossdaddi haus* on her family's property instead of his.

Sarah shook her head, regretting her slip of the tongue. The past needed to remain behind them. Buried. "I'm exhausted, Eli. I need to go home now."

His eyes searched her face, but she kept her expression impassive, her eyes flat.

"Is there something that I should know, Sarah?" he pressed.

Her temper flared again. "*Jah*, in your heart, right there," she poked his chest with her finger, "that's where you should know."

Then she caught herself. What was the matter with her? It seemed that Eli brought out the worst in her when he used to bring out her best. *Ach*, how she wanted that again.

She tried to smile but it turned into a pout. "Never mind, Eli. Forget everything I just said. It's just my tired body protesting. I'm going home now. I suggest you do the same before it gets too dark."

Sarah didn't even glance back over her shoulder as she walked away. If she did, she knew one of them would break down and she'd go back. That, they both would regret.

***

If Sarah admitted it to herself, she'd been waiting for him at the tree. Because that was the same tree where the three of them had carved their initials in the bark so many years ago. Before Eli had shown up, Sarah had searched for the reminder but she'd not been able to find any remnants of the etching. As if that day had never existed.

Throughout the next morning, *nee* matter what Sarah did, whether she tended to the care of the *bopplis*, conversed with Katie, or talked to the visitors who always seemed to be dropping by to see if they could help, Sarah listened for his distinctive knock. Although she knew she shouldn't, she waited for Eli. Waited to hear the sound of his boots walking across the wooden planks of the porch.

And every moment she lingered, she called herself ignorant and loose. By noon, she had graduated to sinner and shameless harlot.

But when Eli finally did arrive, all her self-deprecating chastising went out the window the second she opened the door and he filled it with his presence. Didn't he know to stay away? It was so much easier that way. She wanted Eli to be the stronger one, but it appeared that role now belonged to her, just like temporary foster *mamm* to the twins.

He held out a white box to her.

"What is it?"

"Open it," he answered. "I had to come by today to drop it off and check on my infant friends. How are they doing today? And Katie? How is she settling in?"

Sarah led Eli to the dining room so she could fetch him a glass of Miriam's homemade lemonade that he loved so much. After setting the tumbler down in front of him, she slid into the seat beside his and lifted the lid on the cardboard.

Nestled inside some tissue were two perfect, hand-carved *boppli* rattles. Blue for Samuel and pink for Emma. She lifted the blue one, held it to her ear and shook. A melodic sound tinkled in her ear.

"Oh, Eli. It's so beautiful. *Denke*. The twins are going to love these. Perhaps it will stop Samuel from yanking on the strings of Miriam's *kapp*."

"I had some extra time last evening since I couldn't sleep," he whispered, his eyes locking with hers. She knew why he couldn't sleep. Because she'd suffered from the same malaise ever since she'd laid eyes on him again after so long an absence.

It took a second to clear away the lump in her throat caused by the generous and thoughtful gesture. She raised her eyes to his again, hoping she wouldn't do something humiliating. Like cry.

"This was very craftsman-like of you, Eli," she said in a teasing tone.

His smile bypassed her defenses and landed straight in her heart, setting it on fire. "Some time-honored traditions a carver knows not to trifle with. Every *boppli* needs a rattle made just for them. Even if the twins don't belong to us. Maybe we should go and see if they like them?"

Struggling with the rosy flush that swept across her cheeks, Sarah gently placed the rattle back in the bed of thin paper.

"Let's."

Chapter 12

"You know, Sarah," Miriam muttered, pulling a topic out of thin air, like she was wont to do whenever the mood suited her, "for a man with a thriving business and hardly much time to himself, Eli Troyer certainly does come around the *haus* often enough."

"I noticed that, too," Katie added. "He's so nice. And very handsome."

Even though the heavily pregnant woman's comments were purely innocent, a stab of jealousy still knifed its way through Sarah's chest. She wanted to argue and defend but she fended off the compulsion and remained silent.

It had been more than a week since the twins had landed on Sarah's doorstep. More than a week with *nee* more information or clues than had been initially discovered by the bishop at the bakery in town. And Eli had made a point to stop by each day under the guise of checking on all of them and seeing if they needed anything around the *haus* that a man should be doing.

Though she tried not to, telling herself she was just setting herself up for heartache, Sarah still looked forward to his visits. She couldn't help herself. Like a moth flittering to an open flame only to be incinerated. Her heart would race as she waited for the tell-tale rap on the heavy oak door and then she'd try not to rush to open it so she could gaze upon his face.

Miriam pierced her with a knowing look, so she tried to sound unaffected as she answered. "He comes here to look out for all of us. Three women and two *bopplis* in a large *haus* all alone."

"We were doing just fine before he came back and we'll do just fine again." Miriam puffed out her chest. "We're not helpless. It's not that I don't like Eli and live in gratitude for his kind nature, but we're not useless just because we're female."

Miriam had always been a little bit more progressive than most Amish women of her generation and Sarah delighted in it.

"*Jah.*" Sarah smiled at Miriam's little tirade. "We're not helpless or useless. Most days."

Miriam laughed outright. "I guess you're right, girl. When we're up half the night with a colicky *boppli,* we have every right to be useless the next day. Perhaps anything that involves heavy lifting is best left to the very capable Eli."

With Samuel and Emma finally asleep, Sarah moved about the kitchen, preparing some rolls and jam for an afternoon snack. Even though raspberry was Eli's favorite flavor, he hadn't arrived yet. Sarah gave a shake of her head. She'd already started catering to his every whim.

"Maybe he's afraid we might be so sleep deprived, we'll hurt ourselves doing something we shouldn't," Sarah offered.

Miriam dismissed her suggestion with a roll of her eyes. "If you ask me, Mr. Troyer is just using that as an excuse to come here and see a certain someone."

Sarah stopped pulling the glasses from the cupboard just in time to shoot Miriam a cautionary look.

"Don't give me that look, Sarah Martin," Miriam scoffed. "I've got eyes. And I've convinced my *grosskinner* I have them in the back of my head, too."

The last thing Sarah needed was Miriam influencing Katie to throw her hat in the matchmaking ring, making the two of them a double threat. "I think I'm going to ask Eli to take a look at that shingle that keeps flapping every time the wind picks up. We can't afford to spring a leak and get water damage inside the *haus*. Not with Samuel and Emma with us. When a *boppli* catches the flu, it can be dangerous."

Taking out the pitcher and pouring glasses of the tart lemonade for the three of them, Sarah took a deep breath, growing even more serious. "*Jah*, that part of the roof really should be replaced. I wonder if we ask around at church on Sunday if anyone has any extra shingles on hand. There have been quite a few barn raisings this past year. It would probably only take twenty or so to patch the entire area and make it as *gut* as new."

"After he patches the roof, maybe he can start courting you."

Sarah gasped at Miriam's blunt words and Katie's stifled giggle. "*Nee*. Don't talk like that Miriam. Eli and I are friends and that's what we've always been."

"Not that I didn't love my nephew, but I know Levi was a lot like his *dat*, my *bruder*. Sarah, I'm not ashamed to say it aloud. You married the wrong man."

Sarah stared at the older woman in stunned silence. Miriam had never said anything before, so Sarah had *nee* idea that she'd known about the abusive nature of the Martin men. Had Miriam's *dat*, the elder Martin, been gruff as well? Unable to control his temper? It was inappropriate to ask, so Sarah just waited, hoping Miriam would offer further explanation.

She *had* married the wrong man. Because she thought she could save him. Fix him. Heal the open wounds, both physical and mental, caused by his *vader*. So for now, she frayed her temper and took the safe route. "I married the man who asked me."

Miriam must have spotted the distress in Sarah's eyes. "I apologize, Sarah. That was very forward of me. It appears I'm exhausted again today. I hope you will forgive me."

"Of course." Nothing like an immediate retraction to stir up a tornado of guilt. She laid a hand on Miriam's arm, softening her voice as she stood to walk over to the bassinet. "And I didn't mean to sound harsh in my tone. This is a confusing time for all of us."

"Love will do that to you," Miriam whispered.

Sarah stilled, ears perked. "What did you say?"

"Twice nightly feedings will do that to you," Miriam corrected.

Sarah breathed a sigh of relief. Love wasn't something she was prepared to face right now. When she'd opened her heart to a man, she'd gotten a knife stabbed into it. She wasn't going to open herself up to that kind of pain. The devastating kind that sucked the very breath from your lungs and joy from your soul.

Katie rose, too, and Sarah moved to clean up the remnants of their snack. Sarah's mind wandered to the *bopplis*. She was getting too attached to them, just like she felt the bond growing between her and Eli. Which wasn't in her best interests on either account. A broken heart lay in her future, and she didn't need a soothsayer to tell her that.

As if the older woman could read her private thoughts, she said, "You know, even if their *mamm* comes back for them, it will be a while before she can regain custody of the twins now that the authorities are involved. I'm sure they've been forced to report this situation to social services."

"*Jah*," Katie jumped in. "She could be prosecuted."

Sarah turned to face them both. "Since their *mamm* is Amish and could be in some kind of trouble, I'm sure Bishop Beiler will do his best to avoid any kind of legal action. She's probably just afraid and alone."

Like I am. And like I still feel at least once every single day."

Miriam shook her head. "I don't know about that. When I ran into town yesterday for supplies, I heard talk that the bishop is very upset about this situation. Wants to set an example."

Sarah squeezed her eyes shut against the thought. Her heart went out to this desperate woman, even though she hadn't handled her pain and suffering in an appropriate way. How many times had the darkness of grief and self-blame overwhelmed Sarah until she could have easily done something just as rash to escape it? Throwing this anonymous *muder* in jail was not the answer. What would happen to the innocent Samuel and Emma? How would that negatively shape their lives?

"The bishop said our community is based on family values and this act was the antithesis."

Miriam didn't need to continue, and Sarah wanted to tell her so, but that would be futile. Once her aunt dug her heels in, she'd leave them there until all the skin was scraped from the soles of her feet.

"*Jah,*" Sarah replied in agreement.

"I already love my *boppli* more than anything and we haven't even met yet. I can't imagine anything that could tear us apart and make me want to leave," Katie said, hands clasped in her lap underneath her swollen belly.

Sarah stared at her cousin, so full of joy and hope for the future, even without her *mann*. How could she know about the exhaustion that came with caring for a newborn? The depression that at times racked a body? Sarah wouldn't tell her. These were things that every new *mamm* had to find out for herself.

"As well you should, my dear," Miriam said as she patted Katie's hand. "I love each of my *kinner* more than life itself. I would stand in the road and let a buggy run me down rather than hurt a single one of them. It's the way it should be."

Sarah's mind raced back to the day that Eli had left. Fled their community and escaped her. Wasn't that the same as this *mamm* giving up her *bopplis* because she couldn't handle her emotions anymore? And yet, they'd all welcomed him back with open arms and hearts. It was a double standard that Sarah didn't understand.

"Do you think Eli will return today?" Katie asked.

"Why do you ask, girl?" Miriam said. Probably a little more sharply than she'd intended.

Katie cast her eyes downward.

"Spit it out," Miriam snapped.

"I admit," Katie said, hands wringing in her lap. "I've been afraid at night. I'm not used to being alone in a *haus* with only women. I feel comforted when Eli or Bishop Beiler come to call."

"*Ach*," Miriam said. "I understand and didn't mean to get gruff with you. I've been in this *haus* alone so long with only Sarah to comfort me, I'd forgotten what it's like to have a *mann* around. You'll get used to it. But to answer your question, I don't think we'll be able to keep either one of those *gut* men away, even if we wanted to."

"Do you think Eli is happy to be back in Pride?" Katie asked with real curiosity.

"*Jah*, I do," Miriam answered. "He's always been one of my favorite young men."

Mine, too. Sarah hoped it didn't show on every plane of her face. It had killed her when Eli had left.

She'd ached for him that day. And every single day after.

"He's come back to start afresh," Miriam said. "And that makes him an honorable man in my book."

Sarah didn't understand. "Afresh?"

"*Jah*." Miriam nodded. "I'm sure he didn't come back here to live alone. To be alone. *Nee*. He came back for something. Or *someone*."

Miriam stared at her pointedly, and Katie's smile was so wide it stretched her pretty face.

"I think we both know who that someone could be, don't we, Katie?"

Katie's eyes twinkled with a light to match her grin. "*Jah*, we do."

Sarah saw *nee* reason for this torment and chose not to comment.

A knock at the door caused Miriam to clap her wrinkled hands together in delight. "He's back."

Chapter 13

Still holding the soiled dishes as if in a daze, Sarah walked to the door, opened it with her free hand, then stepped back to allow Eli to come inside. The *grossvader* clock in the foyer chimed the hour. It was three. He was late.

"I thought maybe you weren't coming today," she told him as she closed the door.

"I almost didn't."

Miriam's words rang in her ears. He'd realized that there was *nee* further need to keep coming here and checking on them and was about to tell her this was the last time. Her stomach fell somewhere in the vicinity of her shoes. She braced herself.

"Oh?"

"I almost cut off my finger," he said, holding up his bandaged digit for her inspection.

Sarah hissed in a breath. "Oh, my! How did that happen?"

He looked chagrined. "I was daydreaming. Not paying attention."

She interpreted the unspoken admission. He'd been daydreaming about their previous conversation. The same one that had been keeping her up at night.

"Are you sure it doesn't need stitching?" she asked. "Miriam is well-versed in basic medical skills after tending to so many *kinner* and *grosskinner*. Should I fetch her?"

He shook his head. "*Nee*, it's an injury to my ego more than anything else. I usually pay more attention and rarely hurt myself during work."

He eyed the dishes in her hand. "It appears my injury delayed my arrival for afternoon rolls and lemonade. Is there any way I can convince you to let me have some in spite of my rudeness? I've been dreaming of Miriam's jam. It's better than a Band-Aid or a kiss on the wound from my *mamm*."

Sarah couldn't resist his grin. Or his request. She gestured to the dining room with her free hand. "Miriam and Katie are still there. I'm sure they'll be happy to see you."

He followed along behind her.

"Eli, it's so *gut* to see you today," Miriam gushed. He slid into the seat beside her while Sarah when to the kitchen to get some rolls, jam and lemonade for him. Their voices carried to where she stood preparing the snack.

"What happened to your finger, Eli?" Katie asked, her tone concerned.

"Nothing serious," he laughed. "I just had a little mishap with a band saw. It's not too deep and should heal nicely. Just a tad sore when I bend it. Chores will be annoying for a few days as well as work. Hazard of the trade, I guess."

Sarah stood in the doorway, holding the plate in one hand and the glass in the other. Katie had Eli's hand in her own as she brought it to her face to inspect the bandage. At the sight, Sarah's stomach tightened with a slice of white hot jealousy. *Ach*, what was wrong with her? Katie just wanted to display some empathy and here Sarah was feeling completely inappropriate.

Sarah walked into the dining room and set the dishware down in front of Eli, under the scrutiny of Miriam. Did her baser emotions show on her face?

"*Denke*, Sarah," Eli said, picking up a fork. "This looks delicious. I confess, I'm becoming addicted to your rolls and jam, Miriam."

The older woman chuckled and nodded. "Sure, Eli Troyer. And here I thought that you came here every day because you liked me."

He bit into the roll with gusto and swallowed. "That *is* the reason, Miriam. The great food is simply a bonus."

"Don't fool with an old lady, young man," she fake scoffed at him, but on the outside, she beamed. Miriam had grown as expectant of Eli's visits as she had.

Sarah watched as he took another bite of the roll and jam with the relish of a small boy who'd managed to steal his older *bruder's* toy truck and now held it to his heaving chest in triumph. There was contented pleasure in Eli's expression.

Was it possible to be envious of one of Aunt Miriam's rolls?

"I also admit; I'm becoming enamored of the adult conversation as well." He grinned. "My lathe talks but not in words that I can understand. It's more like bad singing."

"*Jah*," Katie said. "I get it. The more important question is whether or not the wood itself sings to you?"

Eli leaned back in his chair and tented his fingers as he pondered her question. "Katie, I think it's more a fantasy in my head that calls me forward to finish a particular piece. But once it's done... *jah*, that's the part that sings. In tune."

He finished off the last of his roll, the final crumbs disappearing between his lips. She shouldn't be staring, but never seemed to be able to stop herself. He eyed her. She'd retreated to the kitchen and now hovered in the doorway, one foot in the kitchen and one in the dining room.

Miriam spoke before he could comment. "Sarah, quit being rude and get in here. Those dishes can wait until after our guest leaves."

She sank into her chair, averting his gaze. If she didn't, she'd be hard-pressed not to sit there and stare at him until he got up to leave. Now, she didn't just wither under Miriam's watchful eye but Katie's as well. Sarah had never been that *gut* at hiding things.

"So, how are the twins today?" Eli asked. "Usually, I hear them before I see them."

Miriam nodded. "*Jah*, that is true. They're being very *gut* today. Seems they've gotten used to the schedule around here and have settled in."

Eli chuckled as he pushed his plate away. Sarah jumped up to take it to the kitchen. Sitting there, chatting as if nothing was going on between them, set her already frayed nerves to firing. She wanted to get away from him. His proximity sent her into a tailspin.

Sarah could feel Miriam's eyes boring into the back of her dress. Or, were those Eli's eyes?

***

Eli watched Sarah's rigid back as she walked into the kitchen with the dirty dishes. He knew she was avoiding him and the electricity between them. As if running away would make it evaporate into thin air. Didn't she know that avoidance made things even more magnified? *Nee*. Fleeing wasn't going to make this situation any easier on either of them.

His head snapped up to meet the knowing gaze of Miriam. Eli doubted the older woman knew exactly what was happening. In private, she was most likely burying the younger woman under a mountain of judgment and questions. He tore his eyes away from the door to the kitchen. *Nee* reason to fuel the already raging fire. He'd let Sarah avoid him for now.

One of his hand-carved rattles came flying at him out of nowhere, along with an ear-shattering scream. He lifted his hand just in time to make the catch so the rattle didn't go tumbling to the floor.

"So much for their new and improved schedule," Miriam said as she stood to move toward the bassinet. She handed Emma to Katie and she bounced Samuel up and down on her ample bosom.

Miriam pulled her face into a serious expression, purely to get her point across. She continued to soothe the culprit who'd tossed the toy with everything he had in his tiny body. Look out when Samuel stood on his own two feet and became mobile. But he wouldn't be here when that happened. Miriam and Sarah would be breathing a sigh of relief.

"I think Samuel is going to be handful," Eli said. The *boppli* in question was currently using the strings of Miriam's *kapp* as a teething device.

"*Jah*," Katie said with a grin as she gave her pointer finger to Samuel in replacement. The little boy grasped it in an iron grip and squeezed. "Ouch."

Miriam laughed. "I think you're right, Eli. I've known a lot of *bopplis* in my day and this one is very strong indeed. Maybe we better scale back on the midnight feedings before he becomes a toddler overnight!"

"I'm going to take them both to the play blanket and see if I can distract them," Katie offered.

"That's a *gut* idea." Miriam nodded. "It's a really nice day outside, Eli. Why don't you and Sarah go out and sit on the porch. Take the air."

After Katie and Miriam left the room, the silence hung between them. Neither one wanted to comment on the obvious. Sarah's lips were pressed into a thin line and all Eli wanted was for her to soften. He hated it when she was upset and he yearned to ease her pain and discomfort.

"Well, should we?" he asked, choosing not to point out Miriam's matchmaking. "Go outside?"

She didn't answer but followed him to the porch. Her arms crossed, Sarah sank into the wicker rocker and started the chair moving back and forth. Her expression remained hard. As rigid as her spine. Moving slightly back, she glanced into the picture window to catch a final glimpse of Miriam moving down the hallway to the living room. Sarah grimaced.

"Miriam would do better to start minding her own business."

It would have been better if Sarah had remained silent. Maybe he should rise and head for home. Although with his finger throbbing with pain, he really had nothing to return to for today. The shop would have to remain silent while he rested and kept the cut elevated.

"She means well, Sarah. Miriam truly cares about you and thinks of you as family even if you aren't related by blood."

"She meddles in things that are none of her concern."

Eli could tell that continuing the conversation about Miriam wouldn't gain him any ground with Sarah so he tried a different tactic. "She's right about one thing."

"What's that?"

He gestured to the brilliant blue sky, lit by the warm sun. "It's a most glorious day."

"*Jah*," she answered, still rocking furiously. As if doing so would cause the chair to take flight and remove her from the *haus*. From his very presence. "She has a new spirit within her since the twins arrived."

Arrived. Now, there was a strange but empathetic way to describe an intolerable situation. He noted how she avoided stating the facts. The twins had been abandoned. This wasn't a hotel. Eli started to worry that this situation had upset Sarah to the point that she'd lost her grip on reality.

"I think she's enjoying the distraction of caring for them," Eli said. "When one gets older and their family moves on to enjoy their own lives, it can be lonely. Not that she doesn't love having you here living with her, I'm sure. It's just that ..."

"What are you trying to say, Eli?" she asked, her tone dripping with annoyance.

"That *bopplis* breathe life and youth into every situation, that's all. I think they're *gut* for Miriam."

Sarah's swan-like neck stretched as she gazed over her shoulder to avoid looking at him. He'd been dismissed. Sarah had a way about her tonight. She'd become far more authoritative than he'd ever thought her capable of.

"I've noticed that Katie seems to really look up to you," he said, changing the subject again. Not mentioning the name that seemed to spark her irritation. Miriam.

"I'm really enjoying having her here," Sarah said. "I'm looking forward to getting to know her better and determining why she left. She needs to go back home before her *boppli* comes. I'm not going to tell her that, though. I'd prefer she come to that conclusion on her own. I'm surprised that her *mann*, Jacob, hasn't come here to fetch her."

"*Jah*," he observed. He'd thought the same thing. Because if Sarah were pregnant with his first child and left him, he'd move heaven and earth to bring her back home. "I'd wondered about that, too. Perhaps there is more to the story than what we know."

"I think you're right."

To him, Sarah had always been able to handle herself and everyone and everything around her. Especially Levi, who hadn't been easy to deal with due to his abusive upbringing. Eli would never have to play knight in shining armor to her damsel in distress. She wouldn't have expected or tolerated it. Just like now with the situation she found herself unwittingly involved in through *nee* actions of her own.

Chapter 14

"Don't you lie to me, boy," the voice screamed in rage as the belt descended down across his bare flesh. Searing pain came right after the sound of the leather stinging his skin.

Levi huddled in a heap on the plank oak floor of the kitchen, shaking. His *vader* was angry again and he was the oldest, so the anger always got taken out on him. Better him than his frail *mamm* or his younger siblings. Scars peppered his back. Long, jagged, white reminders of what he'd endured since the first time his *vader* had struck him as a gangly ten-year-old.

But he could make it through. Because he had Sarah. His love for her would save him. Make him whole again.

After the final blow had landed and his *vader* had thrown the belt to the floor so he could walk away, Levi laid there. For moments that seemed like hours. His body was battered and broken but not as much as his very soul. He crawled to the front door on all fours and then flattened himself. If he could have, he would have disappeared from view. Disappeared from earth.

Once only silence lingered, he lifted his head and didn't see anything. Careful not to move in a direction that would make his discomfort worse, he rose to his feet. His *dat* would be out in the barn, praying to *Gott* to forgive him for his sins. His *mamm* was hiding. And Levi? He needed to flee to the one person who could help him.

Sarah.

**

Sarah saw the figure huddled beneath the giant oak tree. And she knew. The vicious man had beat Levi again. *Nee* one in their small community knew. Outside of the Martin family. But she knew. And so did Eli. She'd do anything to help her friend. But what could she really do? She was only a teenage girl, not strong enough in body or faith to stop a madman.

Rushing toward Levi, she crouched down next to him and whispered in his ear, "I'm here, Levi. It will be all right."

Tiny dots of blood soaked through the back of his shirt. His right wrist dangled from his arm and appeared broken. A doctor would need to be called to set the bone before it healed with a deformity. Sarah longed to stroke over the wounds and take away his pain. But she couldn't. Couldn't touch Levi.

"*Nee*, Sarah," he answered with a shiver. As if going back in time to relive it again. "I must get away from him. He's drunk again."

Sarah gasped. "Where is he getting the liquor?"

"He's making it himself. It's moonshine."

Sarah slid down to the ground next to him. "What can we do to stop him?"

Levi finally lifted his face. A grimace lit his features but he didn't cry. Levi Martin was far too strong for that. Sarah admired his strength and faith in *Gott* even though his life lay broken around him. If she were Levi, she wouldn't have any faith left within her.

"I'm a grown man, Sarah, and I turn eighteen next week," he said. "I'm going to leave. Start fresh somewhere else. I don't ever want to see his face again."

Sarah didn't think she could reply. What did a friend say to such a declaration? She didn't want Levi to go but she understood how he'd see that as his only option. A deep voice caused both their heads to snap up.

"You don't have to."

Chapter 15

Sarah jolted awake, perspiration on her brow. The dream. It had been so lifelike. As if she'd traveled back in time to that fateful day that she'd agreed to marry Levi, even though she loved Eli. And then Eli had left. Not Levi.

Sarah lay in bed for a few more blissful moments until the scream of a *boppli* caused her to throw her feet over the side of her bed and rise. Rubbing the remaining sleep from her eyes, she stumbled down the hallway to Miriam's room. By the time she got there, Miriam and Katie were already taking care of Samuel and Emma.

Suddenly, Sarah felt useless in her own home. *Nee*. Not her home, not at all. Her home had been with Levi and this was Miriam's *haus*. Maybe she should flee, too. Escape her useless wasted life. And Eli, who carried painful memories around him like a cloak of pain that transferred to her whenever she was in his presence.

From the doorway, Sarah turned and left with Miriam's voice trailing after her. "*Gut* morning, Sarah. Would you like to..."

Nee. She would not like to. Sarah escaped to the kitchen to start the morning meal. And coffee. She'd feel better once she had one cup to chase away the vivid nightmares of her restless sleep. Miriam found her clamoring through the kitchen, taking out her frustration on the pots and pans.

"What is wrong, Sarah?"

"Where is Samuel?" Sarah countered, not wanting to answer the question because she didn't want to lie to Miriam and the truth was unacceptable.

I married your nephew because your bruder used to beat him bloody. Now, I feel guilty because he's dead and it should have been me. I made him hit me. And I made him run to the river with Vernon.

"Katie is changing him and then she's going to call me. We'll bring them down here for their bottles as soon as she's done. I wanted a few moments alone with you. Katie is starting to notice your behavior, and she thinks it's because you don't want her here."

Sarah stifled a gasp. "*Nee.* That's not it at all."

Miriam nodded. "You know that and I know that, but look at it from her perspective. She doesn't know anything about Eli. Your history with him. How his presence set you on edge."

"I will talk to her," Sarah promised. "I can't tell her everything, but I will set her mind at ease."

"While you're at it," Miriam said. "See if you can get her to open up about what happened between her and Jacob. I don't see any reason outside of abuse to break up a family unit. Especially, one that's expecting their first *boppli.*"

"*Jah.*" Sarah nodded as she put plates and silverware on the table. "I agree."

***

Eli almost turned back twice but the clip clop of his horse's hooves continued carrying him forward toward more torment. But then... it was torment of his own making. Something had come over him that day so long ago. Like his voice had been temporarily removed from his body and someone else had looked into the face of the most beautiful woman he'd ever beheld and said, "You should get married."

To another man.

Not him.

And then another tragedy had occurred just a week before the impending marriage of Levi and Sarah, one that could have allowed Levi to escape his violent *vader* without marrying her.

During a meeting of the elders in the community about a possible shunning, the barn roof of the hosting Schrock family had collapsed under heavy snow and ten people had been crushed to death, including their parents. Levi's, Sarah's and his own. Overcome with grief, Sarah hadn't called off the wedding, already resigned to her fate and not wanting to heap even more turmoil on the already floundering Levi. So she'd walked down the aisle the very next Sunday and married the man anyway.

And Eli had left.

So much tragedy for one so young. By then, much of the light had already left her eyes. Those beautiful eyes that used to sparkle with so much joy and life.

And so, even though he wanted to turn back and hide today, he didn't. He'd been upbraiding himself in the confines of his own mind all afternoon as he'd worked on the table he was crafting for an *Englischer* in town. It might be a mistake to visit today, especially in his buggy. But his injured finger still throbbed and he welcomed the excuse to visit the ladies simply because he enjoyed their company. He wasn't used to living alone.

Some cousins had come to stay after the death of his parents and they still worked the farm and lived in the *grossdaddi haus* on his property. But between his work in the wood shop and their *kinner* and chores, he rarely saw them except to wave a greeting.

What on earth are you trying to accomplish here, Eli?

Although he continued to ask himself silent and rhetorical questions, he didn't expect any answers. Because what he'd been trying to accomplish was going back in time and making things turn out differently. Alas, he didn't have that capability. But maybe, just maybe, he could change the future.

He needed to court Sarah properly and he'd start today. Bring her on a buggy ride into town for dinner at her favorite restaurant. It was four in the afternoon and he knew she ate at six. That gave him plenty of time to convince her and still make the reservation he'd made yesterday while on a trip into town. A few blessed moments of sharing each other's company. Would it be so hard, to let himself pretend they were together as a couple and that nothing could tear them apart this time? Just this once?

He was still carrying on his terse, silent argument with his conscience when he saw Miriam's *haus* loom on the horizon.

Eli let out a cleansing breath as he drove the buggy up the dirt driveway. He couldn't recall ever being nervous about approaching someone's home before, but it felt as if everything was riding on her answer. And Sarah's hot and cold attitude toward him wasn't helping to ease his troubled mind.

Maybe because in all the years he'd known Sarah, in all the years he'd approached her in some way, it was always with the understanding that Levi would be there, too. Confidence was a *gut* thing, he observed. You only realized how much you needed it when it faded and was swept away on the light afternoon breeze that now kissed his face.

Calling himself an idiot, Eli got out and hitched his horse so he could mount the porch steps before he changed his mind.

Without Sarah, he felt sadder than he'd been since the death of his parents. Maybe he'd been sad since the first time he'd found Levi huddled underneath the tree, beaten to within an inch of his young life. They'd become fast friends that day and Eli's only regret was that he hadn't been able to protect Levi.

But this was Sarah, whose company he enjoyed. His best friend. *Was* his best friend. He couldn't really claim that part of her anymore. Sarah, who had been a part of almost every *gut* memory of his childhood. She'd been everything clean and decent for both him and Levi. A breath of fresh air in a darkened room. When the ugliness in his own life threatened to overwhelm him, he'd seek her out and the three of them would laugh and play. Talk and dream. Being in a friendship with Sarah made him realize that the world wasn't completely bathed in dark hues, where friends were beaten and the people who could stop it chose to turn a blind eye.

She was part of the light, and he was part of that darkness. He raised his hand to rap his knuckles on the heavy, oak door, listening for the sound of her footsteps. It was always Sarah who answered the door for his visits. Like she'd been expecting him. There might not be a future because she wouldn't step back into her light. But for tonight, there would be a present.

Chapter 16

Hearing the knock at the door, Miriam went to the foot of the stairs and called up, "Eli's here, Sarah. I'll let you answer the door."

Nerves suddenly popped out, as huge as bales of freshly mowed hay and rolled through her stomach just as they'd roll along the field. Could you will the flu? Or a fever? But Sarah wasn't sick. Not of the body anyway. But it seemed that Eli had taken over her mind again like some rampant virus that couldn't be eradicated until it had eaten away all her doubts so nothing was left except to admit how much she still cared about him.

On her way out the door, she glanced at the sunny, yellow quilt on her bed. The one her *mamm* had made by hand to celebrate her wedding to Levi. Oh, how she wished she had her *mamm* today. She'd know what to do. Miriam just couldn't understand even though Sarah knew the older woman tried.

When she reached the top of the stairs, Miriam was down there waiting, bouncing Samuel on her hip. The knock came again and the *boppli* gurgled as he fisted Miriam's apron in his chubby hand.

Sarah took a deep breath and then let it out again before coming down. "I thought in your generation you were supposed to keep a man waiting. Yet here you are, hurrying me."

Miriam guffawed. "In my generation, we didn't beat around the bush. We made our intentions known. I think that's what he's doing. You, I'm not so sure."

"Eli and I are just old friends."

"If that's what you've been telling yourself," Miriam snorted. "You just keep right on lying to yourself, girl."

Sarah nodded because it was best not to argue and stopped to fuss with a fleck of dirt on Samuel's cheek. She hissed in a breath because in that moment, she was overtaken with a memory of Miriam holding Vernon in almost the exact same spot. She shook her head to eradicate it from her mind. But it would always remain chained to her heart.

"Although, friendship is a *gut* place to start." Miriam softened her tone, probably noticing the stricken look on Sarah's face. "Well, go on, Sarah. Let him in so he doesn't walk away from you thinking he's not welcome here this afternoon."

Sarah felt as if she were borrowing someone else's legs as she crossed the remaining space to the door and finally opened it. A tiny, scared voice came out of her mouth. "Hello, Eli."

The look on his face softened her immediately. Happiness to see her, peppered with anguish that she'd taken so long to answer the door. Seeing him now, so handsome and strong, ceased all further worries and thoughts in her head.

"Would you like to go into town, Sarah? For supper?" He asked the questions in rapid succession and she just stood there with her mouth hanging open. Peering around his shoulder, she saw his buggy hitched up and ready to take her.

"Well?" Miriam's steady voice prodded her from inside the foyer. The *boppli's* cooing noises accompanied her aunt's like he wanted her to go as well.

"*Jah*," she found herself saying before she could consider the repercussions. "I'd like that."

"*Gut.*" He raised his eyes to her face and then tilted his head. "Is that a new *kapp*?"

Sarah automatically brought her fingers up to her head to finger the stiff material. She couldn't believe he'd noticed. But then again, Eli's perceptive eyes seemed to capture every nuance.

"*Jah*," she answered. "It is."

She knew she shouldn't have worn this new *kapp* today but she couldn't resist the small gesture of vanity that *Gott* probably wouldn't approve of. Regardless, the fact that he'd noticed caused her heart to sing.

"Let me go back inside and get my shawl." She moved to turn and the shawl miraculously appeared in her hand. Her eyes met Miriam's. The older woman nodded and smiled, giving her unspoken blessing.

Eli placed his hand in the small of her back to lead her toward the buggy. Something in the way he looked at her made her body feel warm all over. This was really happening. They were going on an outing. As if they were courting. Were they? Sarah nearly melted as Eli took her shawl and placed it gently around her shoulders, grazing her arms with his fingertips in the process.

Finding her voice, she glanced back over her shoulder at Miriam. "Thanks for allowing me this evening to go out, Miriam. I'll be home early. And I'll take over the midnight feedings this eve."

"I won't hold you to that," Miriam called after her as Eli helped her up into the buggy. "There's *nee* need to get home early. Just use this opportunity to enjoy yourself. I know you haven't had much of that since... well, just have a *gut* time!"

"We will do that, *denke*, Miriam," Eli called out and backed the buggy away from the *haus*. Sarah liked the way his arm had stayed wrapped around her as he'd ushered her down the porch steps to the waiting vehicle.

Embarrassment harnessed her, holding her immobile in its grip. Could Miriam have been any more obvious?

"Are my cheeks rosy?" she asked in a small voice.

Slowing the horse to a walk so he could turn toward her, Eli pretended to take a closer look at her face, then chuckled and shook his head. "You look really *gut*, Sarah. Your cheeks have a very healthful look to them."

The sound of his laugh helped to ease the butterflies flitting through her stomach.

But not much.

***

The view from the Southland Supper Club was spectacular. The Ohio River cut a swath through the muddy banks below them. The trees were in full bloom with lush, green leaves. Wildflowers the exact shade of her eyes sprinkled the hillside. And Sarah's blooming cheeks were as colorful as the foliage beneath the window of the booth for two right next to the massive picture window.

Eli frowned. She'd hardly touched her pan-seared walleye and he knew she loved it. Her favorite fish. "I don't remember you not having a healthy appetite. You're eating like a bird."

It wasn't that the food wasn't fabulous, because it was. He guessed nerves were getting the better of her just like they were for him. He hadn't finished his steak either, but he'd just box it up and have it for breakfast with some fresh eggs over easy.

"Actually, that's an old wives' tale. Depending on the avian creature, they can eat up to their body weight or more in a day. Birds eat quite a lot." She took the conversation in a completely different direction, and he realized how much he admired her wit and personality in addition to everything else.

Taking a sip of his water, Eli laughed at her and shook his head. "Ah, I remember."

Just to the right of them, the band began to play a low, haunting song and Sarah's head swayed to the rhythm. He knew how much she loved music because when they'd been teenagers, she'd looked forward to the Sunday singings very much. Her singing voice was lilting and clear. He sounded like a dying cow.

"Are you still talking about the birds?" Sarah asked.

"*Nee.*" He smiled. "I'm talking about you always correcting me. But then again, I'm usually wrong. But, you've never hesitated to let me know it and you did that a lot when we were growing up."

She'd been fearless in the expression of her opinions and so unique for a girl, and Eli was all right with that. He didn't like a simpering woman who didn't know her own mind and couldn't speak her truth. His body jolted. Why had he chosen Mary as his *frau* then? He'd treated her as if she were a cheap replica and she'd been nothing but wonderful to him, albeit a bit meek.

She'd gone along with everything he wanted, asking him multiple times a day how she could make his life easier. It had become so cloistering. Like the walls were closing in on him. Not only was he responsible for his own emotions, he was also accountable for *hers*.

"I'm sorry if I did that," Sarah said with a shake of her head.

"Didn't your *mamm* ever tell you that always pointing out when a man is wrong might damage his fragile pride?"

She raised her own glass and took a small sip of her water. "From where I sit, you're feeling just fine about yourself. And my *mamm* told me to have faith in *Gott's* path and the rest would follow. She just wanted me to be happy."

"So do I." He reached across the table and covered her hand with his. The heat between them radiated from his palm through to hers.

Her touch strengthened him. Made him feel like he could do anything. Take on the woes of the world and win.

"I always liked your *mamm*," Eli said with a twinkle in his eye. Her parents had been so loving. Really *gut* people. He leaned over the table. "I know Miriam's a poor substitute."

A vague shrug rippled along her slender shoulders. Losing one's parents and then your *mann* and *boppli*, well, he couldn't even imagine.

"Not a day goes by that I don't miss them. *All* of them."

He could well understand that, losing his own in the same accident and then Mary to illness. "I know."

He set his mouth grimly. He had wanted to keep their time together light and fun, not tumble off the cliff into the morose. They always seemed to drill so deep in conversation. But then, they'd both been through way too much considering the short amount of years they'd been living.

"I know you do. That's why I need you to understand why I still married Levi even after his *dat's* death."

Chapter 17

"Why did you?" he asked, caring too much about the answer. Eli warmed to the memories, finally allowing some of them to infiltrate his defenses. He'd probably spent too much time with Sarah when they were younger. Because now, well, she'd burrowed underneath his skin and he never wanted her to leave. Looking back, he supposed he'd sought emotional asylum with her.

"I felt as if I had no other choice. But being so young and in the throes of grief, perhaps I just didn't see all of them."

"As they say, youth is wasted on the young. But what I liked most about our childhood was that your family always did the right thing," he said softly. "And you cared so deeply for each other. Mine appeared to be so but there was always tension. And Levi's... we know how that one turned out. Without my faith in *Gott* and his path, I might believe that Levi's *dat* had been taken to heaven on purpose. So he didn't hurt anyone weaker than him ever again."

She reflected for a few long moments before speaking. "*Jah*, I've thought the same thing. Levi's *dat* was a very mean man and *nee* one deserves to be treated the way Levi was. My family was so *gut*. I'm very blessed. I never had to live in fear. Every time my *mamm* looked at my *dat* is was with respect and admiration and not ferocity."

He thought of Levi. Eli's friend had borne the scars on his body very well but not the scars of his soul. Judging from her parted lips and narrowed eyes, Sarah had more to say on the subject.

"There's more, Eli. Something I haven't told you. The day that Levi and Vernon died, he..." She squeezed her eyes shut and didn't continue. Eli stroked the inside of her wrist with his fingers, imparting strength. The strength for her to continue.

"*Jah*?"

"He hit me, Eli."

Eli couldn't help but gasp and lean back, taking her hand with him. There wasn't any way he'd release her after that shocking revelation. "He struck you?" He couldn't keep the incredulousness out of his tone.

"*Jah*," she whispered, eyes downcast with shame. Her visible reaction to the words angered Eli. She had nothing to be ashamed of. Levi had struck her. There wasn't anything she possibly could have done to evoke a violent reaction from her own *mann*. And Eli had left her. If at any time, he'd even thought that Levi might turn into his *vader*, he *never* would have left her alone with him. She had to know it and know it now.

"Sarah," he said in a soothing tone. Far more calmly than he felt. Because inside, rage nipped at every nook and cranny of his chest cavity. "If I had known that Levi was capable of hitting you, I *never* would have left Pride."

"I didn't even know, because I never considered it," she whispered with a voice that quavered with emotion. "Not until that day. The day they both died."

He continued to stroke her hand, even through the tears that welled in her blue eyes. "Why don't you start at the beginning?"

"I'd just finished the breakfast dishes and Levi and Vernon were playing in the living room. The *boppli* had been fussy because he was cutting his first teeth, and Levi really did a great job of soothing him. I never worried about him with Vernon. He was determined to not be like his own *dat* with our *boppli*. To be more like my *dat*."

Eli nodded, but he couldn't help stating the obvious. "Probably not like my *dat* either. Yours was the best *mann* by far."

Eli's parents were a sore topic for him so Sarah kept her reply light and Eli was grateful for her ability to correctly read the situation. His *dat* had been cold and unloving. Strict. Quick with a rebuke. "They liked you, too."

He warmed to the memories of her family, letting them in. He'd hung around her *haus* so much they'd liked to joke about him being like the son they'd never had. Sarah had only two sisters. Looking back, he'd probably sought their warmth, support and comradery and so had Levi.

Eli nodded at her neglected plate. "Well, since you're not eating, would you like to dance?"

She stopped tapping her toe and stared at Eli. "*Nee*! We can't dance. What if someone sees us and tells Bishop Beiler we were out dancing in public?"

He grinned at the surprise in her eyes. "Since the band's here and they're playing, I thought that now might not be a bad time. What's the worst that could happen? Bishop Beiler comes by your *haus* and tells us never to do it again? I think he has his hands too full with finding out who abandoned Samuel and Emma to be worried about you and me out to supper. Besides, after what you're doing for the *bopplis*, I don't think even the most severe elder in our community would begrudge you this small happiness."

And I so want to hold you and chase your pain away.

Sarah shook her head and visibly trembled. "The worst that could happen is that I could be considered for a shunning." Her eyes widened, and she looked down. Then, she peered up at the band and her toe started tapping again in time to the lively music.

Finally, he stood and reached out his hand. "Come, Sarah. Take a chance for once. Like you did back when we were kids. That Sarah was brave and fun-loving."

***

Jah, Eli Troyer. That was the Sarah who hadn't been married to Levi Martin. Who hadn't seen more tragedy than a one person should bear.

In all the time she'd known him, he'd never asked her to do something so dangerous, so rash as to dance together in public when they weren't married or even officially courting. Not that she hadn't fantasized about it countless times. But right now, she wasn't sure that she could. "You're really asking me to dance with you? Can you even dance?"

"*Nee*. But I've heard you just sway and let the music be your guide. Just like at one of the Sunday singings," he said with a laugh, clasping her small hand in his large and warm one.

She shook her head as if to chase away unspoken recriminations.

"I'm sorry, it's just that..." She stopped, collecting herself. Since he valued the truth so much of late, she decided to indulge and tell him why she stammered like some confused, adolescent schoolgirl. "You've *nee* idea how many times I used to imagine that you'd ask me to dance."

"Used to?" he asked, face a mask of confusion. "I like to think you still keep me in your thoughts."

Sarah considered the possible outcomes for seconds that passed by in tense silence. Finally, she opted for the truth. "I do."

"You really do?"

"*Jah*, I do." She raised her eyes and narrowed them. Not believing his confusion. "It appears you don't have any idea about a lot of things."

She'd cared for him once as something more than just a friend. She still did.

"Such as?" he asked.

Sarah bit her lip, then let the words tumble free. "I had feelings."

They stood staring at each other. A standoff while the lilting notes of the music wafted behind them.

"You? Feelings?"

"*Jah*."

He still looked as if he couldn't accept it. But wasn't that what this outing was all about? Some warped attempt to get her to admit to things he already knew deep in his heart were true? There couldn't be any mistaking her meaning. Her feelings. It had to be written all over her face.

"And that was...?" He whispered the question. Moving closer.

Closer.

So close that their faces were mere inches away from each other, their lips lush and pleading.

Sarah leaned back. Afraid of the heat between them. She'd just reached the end of her embarrassment tether. Nervous, she forced herself to stop the twirling tide of emotions. "What is this, you buy a girl some supper, distract her with talk of illicit dancing and then expect her to give you all her secrets?"

Well, that's just fine, Eli Troyer, take it all then.

Eli withdrew. "I didn't mean..."

She couldn't leave him wondering, but she could leave it in the past in order to protect herself. "Well, all right, I guess you're entitled to know. You would have known if you'd paid even the tiniest bit of attention. I had the biggest soft spot for you. Never for Levi."

"You did?" His reply was more of a stunned repetition of the question. Once they reached the middle of the dance floor to the shocked looks of the other couples, Eli placed his arms loosely around her. Even though she wished he'd pull her closer in the manner of the *Englisch*, he was respectful and concerned for her reputation and feelings as always. One part of her admired him for his restraint but the other became annoyed with him for being able to keep himself apart from her when this was his idea.

She didn't know whether to be amused or not. "I did."

"Did you ever tell Levi about any of this?" They stopped moving for a moment in order for his probing eyes to search her face. "It didn't have anything to do with his actions, did it?"

She shook her head as they returned to moving in time to the lilting music. The feel of his arms around her, even though they weren't tight enough, made her swoon and her head fill with fantasies of what it would be like to be married to this man and never have to worry about whether or not it was wrong to touch him. Married to the right man this time. "*Nee*. Although my *mamm*. Well... she figured it out."

He smiled. "I'm not surprised. She knew you very well. What you revealed and what you attempted to hide. You've never been that *gut* at hiding things, Sarah. Until now."

Chapter 18

"And I had to get my feelings out somehow – that's why I went back to our tree almost every day. Alone."

Sarah had kept her feelings for Eli locked up deep inside faithfully during her teen years and into her adult years. She'd stopped the day before she married Levi. Because continuing to feel things for Eli constituted a betrayal of the worse kind. Looking back, she wondered if that had been some sort of sign she'd deliberately ignored.

The conversation had spread to serious ground, becoming strained. But they were masters at skirting the real issues and delving deep into dirt that shouldn't be roused, lest it become a dust tornado swirling around them both, covering them in the grime of the past.

Eli leaned in closer and nuzzled her bare cheek. "I thought you went there to read – I was wrong."

She looked at him for a long moment. "*Jah*, you were. About a lot of things."

When he'd opened the door with what he probably thought was a harmless question, he'd actually released a flood of revelations. "Meaning?"

She might as well clear the air about as much as she could. But she would keep back the most important part. "Leaving town like that, so abruptly. Aunt Miriam seems to think that it was because of some arrangement you'd had with your *dat* before he died to apprentice in another city. Was that it?"

"*Nee*, by then my *vader* and I weren't really speaking. He was obsessed with the furniture business and once he'd utilized me as his apprentice, he hardly knew that I was alive except to tell me how I did everything wrong. I don't think he even realized I'd left Pride for several days. It wasn't as if we ran into each other a lot. He tried to avoid my *mamm*. His family. He rarely even came out of the shop for meals."

Miriam had uttered a few choice words about Eli's *dat* but Sarah wasn't about to slice open an old would that might not have completely healed. "All right, if you didn't leave because of a new apprenticeship, why did you leave?"

He didn't answer, just nodded toward the band. Sarah understood the torment that bubbled beneath the surface of a lack of closure. "The music stopped."

But she remained where she was for the moment, looking at him. "So you know your reasons and yet you don't want to tell me. Don't you trust me anymore, Eli?"

"Let it alone, Sarah." Placing his hand on the small of her back, he ushered her back to their table. "You're not the reason and that's all you need to know. Besides, it was too long ago to worry about now. They're gone. They're all gone. We should be focusing on ourselves and those around us who are still here for us to worry about. Like Samuel and Emma."

Stunned and momentarily speechless, she sank down into her seat again. She had nothing to do with his leaving? "Well, I guess that certainly puts me in my place, doesn't it? I apologize for overstepping, Eli. I thought it would be all right, since you're always the one drilling deep and forcing me to express myself."

Words had never been his best method of communication and that trend had certainly continued throughout what she had hoped would be a delightful evening. "Sarah, I didn't mean ..."

Sarah cut him off, not wanting to indulge him and another ridiculous attempt at evasion. "Didn't you? You tell me that we're friends, and then you tell me to leave it all alone and move forward. What if there isn't anything to move forward to, Eli? What then?"

Telling him the truth might kill the very friendship she was now throwing in his face.

"Sarah?"

Living with Levi had taught her how to withdraw into her shell. "Sorry, maybe I expected too much. Maybe I just expected you to be honest with me." A flood of emotions threatened to overflow the banks and drown her. She could feel them swirling inside. A tempest. "But if Levi couldn't be a *gut mann*, maybe you wouldn't have been either. It all worked out for the best. I'm meant to be alone."

***

The conversation was swiftly moving in directions Eli didn't follow. "Levi? What has he to do with it? Why wasn't Levi honest with you?"

He saw tears beginning to pool in the wells of her azure eyes. She quickly glanced away and blinked several times. He reached out and tilted her chin up again so she was forced to look at him.

In a hoarse whisper, she said, "Why do you always treat me as if I'm some weak, pathetic widow who can't look out for herself? Who can't handle her own emotions?" Sarah demanded, finally managing to pull herself free. "Why not just tell me the whole truth?"

"Because you might not like the truth."

Some of the anger left her voice, softening it. "Why don't you let me decide that?"

He couldn't risk it. Couldn't tear away the one *gut*, decent thing that had been a part of his life, his fantasies of his perfect life. That was why he had left to begin with, because he was afraid that jealousy would get the better of him, outweighing his friendship.

"Because it wouldn't be fair to you. It's bad enough that..."

She waited for him to continue, but he didn't. "Bad enough that what?"

He only shook his head. Confession was not always *gut* for the soul. Sometimes, it hurt more than it healed. "I *nee* longer wish to discuss it."

"There you go again, keeping things from me. Is that a thing with you men? Thinking we're beneath you so that we're not worthy of the truth. Afraid we'll cry and create an emotional scene to make you uncomfortable? Well, I'm already crying and emotional, Eli, so it's not going to get any more dramatic for you this eve."

Sarah's conversation of late had been all over the board. If something troubled her, he wanted to know. *Nee* one was more important to him than Sarah. "What are you talking about? And what was it about Levi's inner torment that he wouldn't tell me back then? He was my friend and he shared everything with me. I'm having a hard time digesting it."

He noticed that they were garnering curious glances from a couple a few tables over.

She swiped at her eyes with her napkin. "I don't want to tell you because you and Levi were friends and because... because I couldn't stand it if you thought there was nothing wrong with it. With what he did. How he chose to behave as my *mann*."

Why did she ever think he would take Levi's side? It was never acceptable to raise your hand to a woman. A *gut* man would never even consider it. The fact that Levi had done so made him not much better than his violent *vader*. Eli couldn't condone Levi's behavior, and Sarah shouldn't even be questioning his integrity by withholding information under the umbrella of that flimsy excuse.

Eli felt more lost than ever – and more determined to find his way. "If you want me to understand, start at the beginning."

"I can't. I don't know when it all started. It was just a feeling. A certain look he'd give me like he wasn't quite all there and suffered from a mental affliction."

"What kind of looks?"

"Like he didn't really see me or Vernon."

Eli stared at her. Could it be possible? Did Levi have some type of mental illness after all the years of severe abuse at the hands of his *vader*?

"What?"

"Telling me how much he hated me. That I was ugly and worthless. Meaningless to him. That he'd take Vernon away from me. Raising his hand to me." The tears were back again so Eli raised a finger to run it down the length of her flushed cheek. "But he never connected until that day. Until that day that he died and took my *boppli* with him. To punish me. To make me suffer for being such a bad *frau*."

Any words would be inadequate and taste too bitter on his tongue so he simply placed his warm palm on her jawline as she cried, wiping each errant tear away with the pad of his thumb before it could travel too far.

Of all the things she could've said, this was something he wouldn't have predicted. Levi had been crazy about Sarah. Levi's all-encompassing love for her was one of the reasons Eli had stepped away, because he was so certain that Levi would adore her the way she deserved and take care of her until one of them drew their last breath. Who could have known Levi's last breath would come so soon after and that he'd never placed Sarah on the pedestal where she belonged?

Because he'd never had the male role model he'd needed in order to pave the way.

Eli felt a sense of betrayal, for her as well as for his own beliefs. "Levi called you names? Made you feel like a bad person? A bad *frau*?"

She heaved in a shuddering breath, stemmed the flow of tears and begin speaking again. "I see you are beginning to understand. I know it is a lot to digest, especially when you never saw that side of him."

"How many times did this happen, Sarah?" He still couldn't make himself internalize it, truly take it in along with the implications behind the information. "What exactly did he say?" Maybe it had only been in her imagination, her overcharged emotions. But he'd never known her to be the accusatory type. Not unless that blame was justly deserved. Like when he'd left her.

"When wasn't he mean to me? It started the day after we married. I tried to be quiet, Eli. To make myself so silent it was as if I didn't even exist in my own home. But he wouldn't leave me alone at night and soon I became pregnant. An even bigger burden. When Vernon was born… it began in earnest. Vernon had been a fussy *boppli* right from the start. Always loud. Always demanding. I couldn't disappear anymore. He berated me for not being able to take care of his son. For not being able to take care of him."

Sarah glanced at him pointedly, the candlelight illuminating the sadness peppering her eyes. A torment so deep he wondered now if she'd ever be able to recover.

It still seemed unreal to him. He'd never heard Levi Martin say a cross word to anyone over the course of all the years he'd known him. They'd been best friends for years. "Levi? Levi accused you of being a bad *mamm* to Vernon?"

Why couldn't he accept it? But then, he already knew that answer. Because if he accepted it, his leaving meant even more than it had just a few short moments ago when it had been the worst thing he'd ever done in his life. He'd left her.

Left Sarah.

To be abused by Levi.

The fear began to form within him again along with its best friends, shame and blame. Fear that she'd never forgive him. Why should she? What he'd done was unforgiveable.

Sarah's voice dripped with disdain. As if the words she uttered were covered with battery acid and were about to eat the flesh of her tongue. "Every breath he took, I feared. Would he hit me? Would he kill me? Would he harm Vernon? Until the day that he did. Every fear I'd prayed to *Gott* about for the entire length of my marriage came true. How can I not blame myself? Something I did, something I said. And every night, I still pined away for you, Eli. Even though I know that it's my inappropriate and illicit feelings for you that caused *Gott* to ruin my life! I was being punished then, and I am being punished still. *Ach*, Eli, just take me home."

After he paid the tab, they went outside, and Eli helped her into the buggy.

Words were inadequate to express the emotions roiling through him. Because she was right. Not about her part in it. But about *his*.

Chapter 19

Sarah was in the middle of getting ready for a small get together with her friends and their *kinner* in honor of the *bopplis'* first birthday. Two months had gone by and still *nee* sign of their *mamm*. Sarah and Miriam guessed at the official date but had decided to select three months past the anniversary of their arrival, since they'd gleaned they were about nine months then.

Sitting at the kitchen table with Levi, the *bopplis* asleep in the bassinet, she paused to look him. She was cutting out a squadron of forest animals on pieces of colorful construction paper. They'd be used as simple decorations on the table and the younger *kinner* could always play with them or amuse themselves with the designs.

The strings of her *kapp* kept falling into her face as she concentrated on wielding the dull scissors, and she kept pushing them back, only to have them fall again, obstructing her vision.

"You know, I forgot about this."

She spared him a quick glance, then looked back at what she was doing. She'd already finished a set of paper dolls hooked together by their paper limbs. "Forgot about what?"

"Forgot about how much you enjoy having an excuse to have friends over. To light the *haus* with community and laughter. It's one of the things I like most about you. You're a *gut* friend, Sarah Martin. To everyone."

The entire area was covered with paper, fabric, string and paste. Until half an hour ago, Katie had been beside her, making things to use as decorations, but Sarah's cousin had gone to assist Miriam, leaving them alone.

He leaned over and pushed back the wayward string behind her ear so she could stop blowing it out of the way. "About how overboard you can get when it comes to holidays and birthdays."

"I do not go overboard," she sniffed. "At least Miriam doesn't think so. She encourages me in my endeavors."

"*Jah*, you do," he told her finally, finishing up a string necklace. He took a second to admire his work before starting in the next one. "Don't you think this is a bit much for a one-year-old?"

"*Jah*, it would be considered a choking hazard." She laughed at his ignorance. "Let's keep those to the side for the older *kinner*. I can't wait for Thanksgiving to come. And I'll show you overboard. I make so many paper turkeys with my handprints, Miriam begs me to stop."

"How many did you cut out for last year?"

"She'll probably stop me again," Sarah protested. "But before she did, I cut out about a hundred or so. Miriam finally guilted me into quitting by tallying up how much it had cost for the supplies. I had them in every room. It looked very festive."

He raised a brow as he glanced away. "Aren't you getting Thanksgiving confused with grade school, Sarah? Seems you're trying to go back and relive your childhood years?"

"*Nee*. Believe me, I don't want to go back." Sarah grinned impishly. "Maybe you should brace yourself."

He looked at her, searching her face for clues as to her meaning. "For what?"

"For Christmas – and to be utterly taken in." She went all out for Christmas, starting at the very beginning of the month and making cards by hand for every person in their community. Since the Amish didn't decorate traditionally, making cards, candles and simple wreaths kept Sarah busy for a month. She truly loved making gifts from her heart and seeing the joy on the faces of the recipients.

"That happened the first time I saw you, even though I was far too young to understand what was happening."

It took Sarah a moment to realize Eli referred to her comment about being taken in. She blushed and cast her eyes downward. She remembered that day, too.

He teased her like he was wont to do with a wink and a grin. "We went to school together. How could you remember such a day and so many years ago?"

"But I do." Carefully, he completed his task.

She stopped cutting, mystified. "How could you possibly remember that far back?"

Even though I do, too.

"I remember." Then, because she'd given an incredulous response, he seemed to want to prove it to her. "You kept questioning the teacher about the color of the lilacs in bloom. He said purple and you insisted they were lavender."

Sarah smiled in response. "Most lilacs were then, and still are, lavender."

"How would you know the official lilac color chart?" He sent her a smug look. "Ever been a botanist?"

No." That had nothing to do with it. Lilacs were her favorite flower, and she didn't care what any dog-eared, outdated textbook had to say.

Lavender.

"And don't pretend you don't know about the white and royal purple either," he chuckled. "I know you consider yourself a connoisseur of all things lilac. Besides, it was a harmless enough thought then. And still is."

"*Jah.*" She glanced up at him. Happy to be sitting here beside him in easy conversation. It just felt so right. "I do love all the colors but *lavender* is my favorite."

"There. Done," he pronounced, with a flourish.

He did nice work, she thought, surveying his long chain of paper dolls. Reaching over to the three rolls of crêpe paper closest to her, she presented them to them. "Right now, Aunt Miriam would like you to start braiding these together for a makeshift tug of war." She pointed vaguely around the room, leaving it up to his imagination. "We'll do it outside on the soft grass with the older *kinner*. In case someone falls. I don't want to use real rope because it tends to burn their tender skin and leave rope slivers."

Eli looked down at the rolls dubiously. "I doubt this was truly Aunt Miriam's idea, Sarah." He looked around at all of the breakables present inside Miriam's. "And outside is a *gut* idea, too."

She grinned. "*Jah*, I wouldn't be able to forgive myself if I were responsible for random scrapes and bruises."

"You know," Eli said, twisting the three strands together awkwardly, "this isn't exactly a major holiday. It's a birthday event for two *bopplis* not even old enough to understand." Two of the rolls fell from his hand, unraveling as they went. "Aren't you worried about censure from the older women?"

Sarah stooped to retrieve the crepe. Holding one, she quickly retrieved the other, making her way to Eli. "Of course not. It's a birthday for our adopted *bopplis*. Wouldn't you expect the same?"

"Same as what?" he wanted to know.

"Some type of observance of the day *Gott* granted you entrance into this world and set you on your path." She thrust the roll in his hands and began rewinding the pink one.

"For my birthday, I wouldn't want any fuss," he grumbled.

She raised her eyes to his. "*Jah*, I remember." And then a smile captured her mouth and turned her lips upward. "Now tell me if I ever listen. I do remember when your birthday is, Eli."

Because every memory involving you is burned on my brain for all eternity.

The conversation and his surly attitude about life events evoked more memories. Sarah loved making cards for birthdays just like she did for Christmas. She'd taken special care with Eli's. Each and every year, she'd been blessed to have him in her life serving as her friend. Except for the few he'd been gone and she didn't have his address.

"No, I can't say you ever did forget it." He surveyed the room and continued with his crepe paper braid. "You're really going to do more for Christmas? I can't imagine a card for every person. It's hundreds, Sarah."

"*Jah*. I plan to start gathering supplies the middle of October, but if the *bopplis* are still here ..."

"Couldn't you just do one per family?" he countered. "You're right. If Samuel and Emma are still here, they'll be walking. Can you imagine their curious and grubby little hands all over your paper supplies?"

At his innocent comment, a wave of melancholy washed over Sarah. Vernon had never made it to his first birthday. As a *mamm*, she'd never experienced a toddler. Would she be able to be the foster *mamm* Samuel and Emma deserved? *Gut* thing she had Miriam to lead the way.

She stared at him, not sure how to respond. Not really wanting to discuss why she'd allowed the waves of sadness to pervade her positive mood. "*Jah*, they'll be a handful to be sure."

He snorted. "A handful with tiny, grabbing hands. Touching everything and putting it in their mouths."

He had her there. "I'm really grateful for Miriam. You'd be amazed at how much of the childcare she still does at her age. She hasn't slowed down a bit."

Reunited with the second runaway roll of bright blue paper, he began twisting the braid again.

"You're very lucky to be able to live here with Miriam," he said, nodding but soon course corrected. "But that doesn't mean I think you're not capable of living alone. You could have done that too and been just fine."

Ach, he must think her a waspish shrew of late, ever since their evening out. Poor Eli was always quick to defend himself before she could even get around to attacking him. She needed to stop doing that since her behavior was clearly causing him to feel uncomfortable.

"I don't like being alone in a big *haus*," she agreed. "This living situation is *gut* for both of us. And now, with Katie here, for her, too."

"Agreed." His fingers were getting pink and blue from the crêpe paper. Eli wiped them on his pants and continue twisting the strands. "Do you think Samuel and Emma are even going to know what's going on?"

It was as if someone had siphoned all the fun out of the Eli she had known. Even if the *bopplis* didn't remember any of her efforts, she couldn't allow their first birthday to go by without marking the occasion. "You must be a regular joy to be around when Christmas comes, Ebenezer. Tell me, what did Iowa do to you? Didn't they have any celebrations there?"

Chapter 20

A knife twisted in Eli's stomach. Living in Kalona had only honed his attitude. That and Mary. She'd never been keen on celebrating much of anything, content to sit home and bake or knit. Mary's eyes had never sparkled with curiosity and vitality like Sarah's did. And lively conversation? Well, that had never materialized. It was like he'd gone out and deliberately selected a *frau* who was the antithesis of Sarah. As if doing so could help him to outrun the galloping emotions he felt whenever his memory returned to her.

"Nothing out of the ordinary. But living there opened my eyes a little bit more," he told her.

She shook her head, taking the crêpe paper rolls from him. He was creating ropes that were too tight and could burn the fingers of the *kinner* holding them just like the real rope she'd been avoiding. Quickly, she began to braid the three strands together. Long chains began to fall from her fast moving fingers. "I don't know about your eyes, but it certainly sucked out your soul."

He hissed in a breath, never expecting to hear something so harsh and laced with animosity fall from her lips. But she was right. He certainly wasn't returning as the same man he'd been when he'd left. Some days, he wondered if he had all of his soul still intact. What he did know was he felt most himself while in her presence.

Suddenly, he wanted to make her smile like before, to wipe away that serious look from her eyes. To erase the thought that he was some soulless shell of his former self.

"I guess it's my responsibility to try to be the best man I can be now that I've returned home."

"Here," Sarah said and Eli watched her hand dip into the bowl on the table and clasp a homemade caramel that Miriam had made. Then, as he began to protest, she popped it into his mouth. "Something to start the process and sweeten you up then."

Eli swallowed and then tried in vain to remove the sticky substance from his molars. "I don't need sweetening, Sarah. I'm a man, tough to the core."

"*Nee*, Eli. I kind of like you just the way you are. Tough men can be mean and ornery." He immediately regretted his flippant comment. Her eyes grew hazy, and he knew she was referring to Levi. Probably thinking back to the day the other man had struck her. *Nee*. She was right. Men shouldn't be tough in that way.

When she raised her eyes to his, the playful expression slipped away from her face. In its place, sudden as a tornado dropping down from a thundercloud, was an urgent longing that twisted all around her. What he saw in her eyes was yearning. The same kind of desire he felt rattling the bars of his own restraint.

"*Gut*." He uttered the one syllable and brought his hand down over hers, relishing her warmth.

Eli used the pad of his thumb to swirl circles around the inside of her palm. Did she have any idea what she did to him? Any inkling of how crazy she made him, sitting here beside him, looking so inviting?

Tempting him with every move she made.

"I thought we were planning for the *bopplis'* birthday, not Saint Valentine's Day," Aunt Miriam quipped as she walked in, carrying a stack of colorful paper she'd found in a box in the attic. She put the box down on the sofa beside the coffee table. "Thought you might want these. Remnants from Sarah's Christmas card extravaganza from last year." Mirth tangled with approval in her watchful eyes. "Didn't realize you were testing the smoothness of Sarah's skin, Eli."

Sarah shot her a warning look. "Aunt Miriam!"

The older woman held up her hand and placed it over her forehead, as if to keep herself from a faint. "Sorry, the temperature in this room has increased to an uncomfortable level. I'll just go and see about feeding the twins. And finding Katie."

"I should help you, Aunt Miriam," Sarah said, rising from her seat at the table.

Miriam shook her head. She glanced over her shoulder at Eli. "I'd say you have your hands pretty full already, Sarah. Not that I can blame you."

If Sarah's cheeks flushed any redder, she was going to spontaneously combust. Eli simply sat still and delighted in the bloom the rosy hue provided her beautiful face. Aunt Miriam probably shouldn't tease her so mercilessly but the older woman's personality didn't provide for anything else. Aunt Miriam was feisty to be sure.

Taking an interest, and welcoming the chance to change the topic and make a quick getaway from the crepe rope braid, he joined Sarah at the bassinet. Eli looked down at the twins. Today, he hadn't even bothered going through the charade of holding Samuel so the *boppli* could tug on his suspenders. They looked well. Soon ready to launch themselves upward and begin toddling on two legs instead of crawling on all fours.

"How are they doing?"

"They're eating well and trying to pull themselves up on the furniture when they're loose on the floor," Sarah replied, bending over to pick up Samuel. The little boy thrashed gleefully as she took him in her arms and inhaled his scent. Samuel gurgled while Sarah bounced him. She pointed to a green stain on his shirt. "Like typical *bopplis*. The food goes into their stomachs, but half of it comes up. We just found out he's not too fond of peas, *nee* matter how we prepare them."

"Do any *bopplis* prefer vegetables?" Eli asked. "How about sweet potatoes? They seem to be the universal food for everyone under the age of two."

"*Jah*," Sarah said with a smile as Samuel fisted the string of her *kapp*. The little guy was about to yank it when Sarah gently extricated it from his small fist. He frowned and looked as if he wanted to cry over it but she soothed him.

There wasn't any denying how much Eli cared about her. Words had passed between them about that, and it couldn't be denied on either side. And yet, she'd only confessed to having had a crush on him in the past. Between the twins and everything else getting in the way of properly courting her, Eli worried they might never get past it and be able to forge a new life. So maybe words were better left unsaid at this point. At least until the issue of the *bopplis* was solved.

Turning, she handed Samuel to him then picked up Emma. "All right, just remember you asked for this," she warned.

Jah, *I did. Because I love watching you with them and imagining they're our* kinner.

"So, what's on the menu tonight?" he asked, following her into the kitchen and looking around. There were two high chairs at the table where two chairs had once been. He was tempted to run his fingers over the worn wood, sure his *dat* had made them years ago. The dining room table, like the *haus*, was from another era and looked out of place beside the high chairs. Eli's eyes widened as he turned to look at Sarah. "*Ach*, you've replaced the chairs with higher ones for the twins."

"Roast chicken and sweet potatoes, and *jah*, I did," Sarah replied, answering both his questions as she moved Samuel to his seat. Eli echoed her movements with Emma. "It's nice that we're giving Miriam this meal off. I know she has some quilting she's been wanting to finish."

"Quilting?" he echoed. "Is she making the blanket for a special occasion?"

"*Jah*," Sarah giggled. "For herself. She says she needs a change. And she loves doing it so much who is going to tell her not to indulge?"

She really was something else. Serious one second and erupting in girlish laughter the next. Eli shook his head. "You want the whole world to be happy."

Her eyes met his. "Nothing wrong with that. Happiness is a *gut* thing."

"*Nee*," he agreed. "Nothing wrong with that."

I just wish it was me who made you happy.

She moved to the stove to check on the two glass jars that Miriam had left warming. "I just wish I had a little more time to clean the storage spaces properly, but I've been so busy. You realize that I haven't even made a dent in the attic where Miriam found these supplies? The whole space seems overrun."

To him, attics were for storing not for cleaning. But then Sarah ... she knew how to run a *haus* and make it shine in every way. He didn't even want to think about what she'd say if she saw his own storage area in the wood shop. "Why don't you just leave the door closed and forget about it?"

She looked at him over her shoulder. "The door to the attic is always closed, silly. But to forget about it? I'm looking forward to it. There are some old crates up there I haven't had a chance to open up yet. I'm saving that for a special treat. Maybe the next day it rains with a solid soaker."

"Treat? Really?" Eli didn't think of rifling through old, musty trunks as something to look forward to. More like something to dread.

"Sure, they're probably full of old memories."

Turning the flame down, she gingerly removed the jars and tested the contents of both by spilling a drop from each onto the inside of her wrist. Satisfied with the temperature, she brought the jars over to the table.

"Maybe Aunt Miriam has treasures she hasn't shared yet."

Eli took the spoon Sarah handed him and picked up one of the jars from the table. "More like secrets. Isn't that an invasion of her privacy?"

"Only if she hasn't given me permission," Sarah said. "Actually, she's the one who suggested it right before the *bopplis* arrived. Miriam knows how much I love rummaging through things, hunting for items to be repurposed. She thought it might take my mind off ... things."

The workings of her mind left him bemused. Coaxing the spoon between Samuel's lips, Eli could only shake his head. "Now that I know that, Sarah Martin. I have three storage areas at my property that are all yours. The storage room in the wood shop is overflowing, and I've never even *been* in the attic."

Emma's appetite was in rare form tonight. Sarah could hardly get the spoon to the *boppli's* mouth fast enough. "Oh, I don't know," she said with a teasing grin. "That sounds time consuming. As well as exhausting."

He smiled too as Samuel finally opened his mouth wider. "You do seem to have a flair for it. Look at all the things you were able to do today with the simplest of supplies. I can't wait for my hand-made Christmas card to arrive. It might be the first Christmas I've actually looked forward to in a long time."

"Oh?" She looked at him.

"*Jah.*" He didn't really need to elaborate because understanding was written all over her beautiful face. She'd enjoy making him a card and he'd delight in receiving it. His first from her. He wondered why she'd never done the making of Christmas cards as a teenager, only birthday cards. Probably too overwhelming to create so many at the same time.

Sarah beamed, then scooped another bite of shredded chicken into the *boppli's* mouth.

He glanced in her direction, seeing her smile. Reveling in it and delighting in the fact that he'd brought it about instead of a frown just this once. "You had to know that."

"Well, yes, I knew," she admitted. "But it's nice to know that it's appreciated. And that what I'm doing is making a difference in someone's life. Especially yours."

"It will, that I can promise," he said, scooping a blob of orange sweet potato off Samuel's face and back into his mouth.

A few moments of silence followed as they each processed the revelations. Using the bib she'd tied on Emma, Sarah cleaned the little girl's very messy chin. "You're doing a great job with him, Eli. Is this the first time you've tried to feed a *boppli*? It can be most tedious."

"*Jah.*" He chuckled. "Seems Samuel wants to wear most of his orange food instead of eating it. Maybe he wants to go as a pumpkin to his own party."

"Like a costume? Too bad it isn't our way to celebrate anything with costumes. I'm sure I could put together something spectacular with my finds in the attic. I've always wanted to wear a costume. Most *Englisch* traditions, I'm fine to forgo, but that one ..."

Eli saw the alert look in her eyes and, too late, realized his mistake at the hands of his loose lips. "Never mind. I don't want you rummaging around up there to put some strange outfit on this *boppli*. Or me for that matter."

"Tell me," she prodded, her lips tugging at the corners. "Would you ever wear a costume if *nee* one but me would ever see you in it?"

Eli paused but then decided to humor her, enjoying the smile the conversation had caused. "Remember back in grade school when we read *Treasure Island*?" he asked, eyes twinkling. "If I could dress up in a costume for one day and not be seen, I'd dress up as a pirate. Long John Silver."

The admission, he realized later, was his second mistake. His first being not shutting the conversation down after he'd uttered the word pumpkin.

Sarah set down the food and spoon so she could clap her hands together. "Really? It's so exciting. Pirates! With a wooden leg, patch over one eye and a parrot on your shoulder?"

Feeling decidedly uncomfortable, Eli watched as Sarah cleaned Samuel and Emma and put the dishes in the sink to be washed later. Had he just opened up Pandora's Box? Sarah looked far too interested in the subject matter. His pirate fantasy might have been one best left in the past.

But anything seemed better than walking around on eggshells waiting for her to reveal her thoughts. And then he saw her mirth, and his about opening up began to change radically. He hadn't realized that while he was struggling with his sense of values and putting on his mask, she'd also been putting on hers. Maybe it was time to take them off.

Chapter 21

Eli contracted a severe case of dry mouth as he surveyed the way Sarah's eyes danced with each sway of her hips. The urge to constantly touch her was simply becoming too strong. He'd walk over a blanket of hot coals in order to be able to continue to see her. Talk to her.

Thinking back to their shocking conversation while feeding the *bopplis*, he hissed in a ragged breath. If she told him to put on a flowy white shirt and breeches, he'd do it. Of course, he'd have to do it in private, because if anyone other than Sarah ever saw him in such attire, he'd be ostracized within the community. Blatant demonstrations of prideful behavior were frowned upon and he couldn't think of many more obvious examples than dressing up as a character from a *kinner's* book. But if he did indulge, would she be attracted to his pirate swagger? He'd have to have some, wouldn't he? The costume alone would elicit rash behavior. He imagined the shocked look on Sarah's face as she swept her gaze over Long John Eli.

"Are you ready?" he asked.

"*Jah*," she said. "I'm really looking forward to going into town tonight. We have a reservation at seven at the restaurant. My choice, remember?"

He laughed. "How could I forget, Sarah? You've been reminding me about it the past three days. I'm starting to think you have something nefarious up your sleeve."

"Hmm," she said, eyes afire with merriment, "I just might."

Eli had just turned to lead the way to her front door and out to his buggy when Sarah grabbed a bag from the hall table. Miriam waved from the staircase.

"I'll see you two swashbucklers later," she called. "Don't worry about Katie and the *bopplis* tonight. I've got it all covered. Take every opportunity to enjoy yourselves."

Eli's eyes narrowed and his heart started to pound. Had his private ruminations conjured a fantasy into reality? "What is she talking about, Sarah?" He posed the question, but he thought he might already know the answer and it scared him.

"What day is it, Eli Troyer?" she asked with a lift of her eyebrows.

"It's Saturday the 30th of October."

"Right," she said. "Remember when you accused me some months ago of losing my youthful exuberance? Of never taking a risk? Well, I've decided I want to take one. Tonight."

Ach. Nee! She was going to ask him to dress up like a pirate. For an *Englisch* Halloween party. What if someone saw them? Found out? What if Miriam couldn't keep the secret?

"Sarah, where are we going?" he asked, tone filled with trepidation. He felt sick.

"To the Halloween dinner and dance at The Ribeye Steakhouse in Jamestown." she explained in a rush. "Don't worry, Eli. It's far enough away that *nee* one will know us there. Besides, we'll be in full costume, complete with masks. Please let me try doing something impulsive. For me. Just this once."

Sarah pulled a tambourine from the bag and gave it a shake. "I've never had one of these before." Tucking her tambourine under her arm, Sarah also pulled out a plastic sabre, complete with scabbard. "For you. To complete your boyhood fantasy."

Why didn't she realize the only boyhood fantasy that mattered to him anymore was *her*?

"Sarah," he said. "Of course, you've never had a tambourine before. Where, might I ask, did you get that one?"

"Miriam."

She didn't expound further, and Eli knew he wouldn't like the answer. Maybe it was best to just concede to this forbidden evening and not ask any more questions.

"My pirate, Eli, has 20/20 vision along with his soulful brown eyes and two *gut* limbs without a peg leg. And as for the parrot, it would definitely interfere when he stopped to swoop up the fair maiden he rescued from the evil ship bearing the skull and crossbones." She grinned mischievously. "But I do have a stuffed parrot along. In case the real Eli disagrees."

"Sarah, there is *nee* way we can hide a horse and buggy at the Ribeye. How do you propose we remain incognito?" he asked, exasperated.

"We will park our horse and buggy at the General Store." She clapped her hands together as if it were already settled, even though her plan lacked logic. "Then, we will walk inside and out the back door. It's just a ten-minute walk to the restaurant on foot."

"On foot in outfits? Sounds more like a befuddled fiasco than something out of Robert Louis Stevenson."

Sarah shrugged nonchalantly. Eli tried very hard not to stare, but her elegant fingers had the tambourine clutched in a death grip and in that moment he knew how important this outing was to her. To witness her excitement disarmed him, to put it mildly. "You have your costume fantasies, I'll have mine."

He looked at her standing beside him. "Is that what this is?" Eli turned toward her, a warm smile on his lips. "A fantasy of yours? To be attending your first costume party with a man wearing white pants, knee-high boots and a shirt with sleeves big enough to hide Samuel and Emma inside?"

"*Jah*," she answered glibly, turning her face up to his. "But only the first of many. What's yours, Eli?"

Oh, Sarah Martin, I can't tell you because it would be considered far too forward.

"To be attending a secret costume party with a woman dressed in a swirling red skirt and a gaily colored scarf jauntily tied at her waist," he said with a wink. "Will there be bobbing for apples and pin the tail on the donkey? I think we should take this all the way if we're going to take on the risk of being discovered. And shunned."

Sarah gasped. "Do you really think we could be shunned just for attending a costume party?"

He pushed back. "*Nee*, but I do think they would gossip about us for years."

"Years?" she asked, her face falling in a puddle of dejected features. "Maybe we should stay here with Miriam."

"*Nee!*" Miriam screamed from upstairs. She'd been eavesdropping. "You will go out. And you will go out now. Eli, take her out the door before I have to come down there and slap her with her own tambourine."

In reply, Sarah raised the instrument in question and rhythmically hit it with the heel of her hand. She shook it so that the tiny symbols all along its perimeter chimed in. "And I'm happy to be able to fulfill your every wish. Let's go before I change my mind."

If only.

Dragging himself out of his mental revelry, Eli looked down at the costume in the bag and wondered if it was going to torment him during the evening. Or if he'd wind up hitting someone with the scabbard. Or if the stuffed parrot would fall off his broad shoulder to become roadkill on the hardwood floors. "My real wish is to get on the road before it becomes too dark and dangerous. It's already five-thirty, and it's going to take a while to get there."

Although the time alone in the buggy with Sarah would be most welcome.

Her grin widened as her eyes began to sparkle with humor. "*Jah*, we should get started right away. *Gut* evening, Miriam."

"Go now, Sarah," Miriam called from above, still firm and demanding.

When Sarah looked at him like that, he nearly swallowed his tongue. Pretending to be oblivious was next to impossible so he didn't even try. "Shall we be off then?"

Her laugh was ebullient as she went to get the long fringed shawl that she'd chosen for the evening. It was far more ostentatious than she'd normally wear so it must go with the costume that he still hadn't yet seen on her. He squeezed his eyes shut. Gott, *help me to get through this evening.*

"*Jah*, let's get going before Miriam decides to make her presence known instead of just her vocal chords."

Opening the front door, Eli pointed toward the sky. "That's a crescent moon."

"So it is." Undaunted, Sarah laughed. "You should see me when it gets full. I'd find something even more daring to do than this."

He resisted the urge to touch her, knowing that if he gave in, he'd regret it. He'd want to turn around and go back home. The temptation of seeing her in whatever outfit she'd planned would be enough. Feeling her skin would be his utter undoing. "You have surprised me this eve, Sarah, do you know that?"

She swept past him, bag in hand and stepped through the doorway. "I'm always surprising you, Eli. And you are going to make us late if we stand here talking any longer."

So much for strategy, he thought with an inward smile. "You know, I really don't want to wear a costume, even if it is a pirate one. But I know how much it means to you."

Calling out a final goodbye to Miriam, who'd volunteered to remain with Katie to watch the *kinner*, Sarah glanced over her shoulder at him. "You really don't want to waste this opportunity to make me happy, do you? Besides, it'll be fun."

Eli frowned. "Only if it truly does make you happy."

***

But, oddly enough, it did.

On the whole, he'd never really cared for any kind of formal gatherings. He'd seen far too many of them over the years. Weddings. Funerals. People milling around, pretending to have fun while making empty conversation as they ate baked goods and drank lemonade. Shy by nature, Eli preferred dealing with people on a one-to-one basis. If it were up to him, gatherings in general would be outlawed. Sarah Martin and her propensity to attend them, would be outlawed.

And yet, he was having a *gut* time, almost against his will.

There was just something about experiencing the evening through Sarah's eyes that lit him up inside *nee* matter how much he wanted to deny that simple truth.

In a way, it was as if he were truly seeing *her* for the first time. This grown up version of her. People seemed to gravitate toward them because she shone so brightly. She took an avid interest in everything and everyone. Being near her just naturally made everything better. His mood included.

He watched as she talked with a local businessman who owned a landscaping company and Eli suddenly found himself growing jealous of a balding, elderly, out of shape man in a Batman costume because Sarah was laughing at something he'd just said to her. Eyes sparkling, head thrown back. Even though the costumes and masks she'd chosen for them were very chaste, and her hair was still bound underneath a scarf, the sight of her out of a plain dress, vibrant in unusual colors, made his heart skip a beat. Those intense hues just brought out even more of her natural beauty.

If anyone had been privy to his mind, they would've said he was in love. He had to do something about that. Sweep it away before it dug in its heals and came to stay.

But not tonight. This night was for enjoying. Cherishing.

"You certainly know how to make friends well enough," he murmured to Sarah as he went to her. The landscaper's attention had been temporarily commandeered by his *frau* dressed as a pilgrim, complete with white lace apron and black buckled shoes. The woman stole the breathless Batman away. Saved by a lady of the Mayflower. Eli handed Sarah a cup of soda, a treat in itself.

She took the red plastic cup in both hands and held it first before sipping. "What do you mean?"

"Everywhere I turn, I see people staring at you. Even men. I don't like it." He nodded at Batman. "The landscaper thinks you're a botanical expert after your speech on the lilac varietals. He's about this far," Eli held his thumb and forefinger half inch apart, "from offering you a position at his garden center designing landscapes for rich *Englischers*."

She blushed a rosy hue but shook her head. "That type of offer would hold *nee* interest for me, as you well know."

Eli played devil's advocate with a laugh. "I'm not so sure, Sarah. The offer may come with lucrative bonuses based on how many lilacs you could get to bloom, not to mention a tempting salary. And you'd be able to escape Miriam a portion of each day."

"I don't need a job, Eli. I have enough to do at home with Miriam and the *bopplis*."

Eli laughed as Sarah brought the cup to her lips. "I was just teasing, Sarah. I know you don't need a job."

Her answer had pleased him a great deal. "You would've been a revelation to my *vader*. He felt that there was nothing more important than work. And money." His mouth hardened as he thought of the countless grudges and blame that had littered his *vader's* life – and stained his *muder's*. Eli looked off into space. "Not even the needs of his family."

He got momentarily lost in the memory of his cold *vader*. Sarah tugged on his sleeve until he looked at her again. "Eli, do you want to talk about it?"

"*Nee*," he said, waving his thoughts away. This wasn't any time to be talking about his *vader*. Thinking about him. The memory left him cold and he just wanted to enjoy this private time with Sarah. He studied her face, looking for some indication whether she was serious or strictly making conversation. "So you're going to be taking care of Miriam for the rest of your life?"

She finished her soda in a last long sip, but continued to hold the glass in her hands, gripping it tightly. "You make it sound insignificant. I care deeply for Miriam."

He hadn't meant to offend her, he just thought that she'd enjoyed being a *frau* and a *mamm*. Enough to give it another try. With him. "Not insignificant, just not, well..." he said for lack of a better word. Actually, he didn't have the appropriate words to articulate what he wanted. Not without putting his heart on the line before he was certain of her response.

Cocking her head, she looked at him, the empty cup dangling from her fingertips. "Keeping a woman company, helping her to run a large *haus*, taking care of someone else's twins, that's not lofty enough a vocation for you? We can't all be as supremely talented in craftsmanship, Eli. Not like you are."

It looked as if he was treading on sacred territory. Eli backtracked. "I didn't mean that."

"I should hope not." She managed to say it before the smile slipped out, betraying her. Eli knew he was off the hook. She teased him.

Her eyes collided with his. "Dance with me again, Eli." She lifted her hands, waiting. "Make me feel as pretty as you made me sound earlier tonight. I so loved it the last time we danced. I want to do it again. To feel your solid arms wrapped around me. Please."

The word please was going to be his sheer and utter undoing. Her lips still turned down at the corners in a becoming pout. He scrunched his forehead and eyed her. Would it be all right to dance again? They hadn't been recognized. In fact, *nee* one in attendance had even bothered with a second look. To the other partygoers, they seemed just another young couple enjoying the event.

He gladly took her into his arms, holding her there. In front of all these people, it was safe. He couldn't do anything that might lead to something forbidden, not here. And if holding her close to him like this constituted sweet agony, so be it. At least he was holding her.

"You don't need a fancy costume for that, Sarah. You are pretty." And then, midsentence, he changed his mind. "No, I take it back. You're not pretty."

She reared back in shock. "I'm not?"

"No, you're not. *Lavender* lilacs are pretty." He leaned his face into hers, whispering against her ear. "Roses are beautiful. And you, Sarah Martin, are definitely a rose. Without the thorns. All right, maybe an occasional thorn."

Eli saw her eyes prick with tears and he knew the compliment had struck true, had meant something to her and that made him feel incredible inside.

"Now you're going to make me cry," she whispered as she clung to his arms. He stayed steady and held her tighter.

She wasn't kidding, he realized. He wished he had a handkerchief, but his costume hadn't come with pockets. "Don't do that. I'll have ten people in the immediate vicinity pummel me to the ground if they see you crying after dancing with me. I think half the men here are already enamored by you. I need to stay in one piece so I can drive the buggy home later. What would Miriam say if I stranded you at the restaurant?"

The entreaty had done the trick, lightening the mood. She laughed. "You say the silliest things, Eli. *Nee* one here would fight you over me. That's ridiculous. I don't have makeup on or my hair down and styled like these fashionable women. And I never will. And as for Miriam... well, she'd never give you any of your favorite raspberry jam ever again."

He smiled into her eyes, remaining serious. "Your beauty runs so much deeper than what can be seen on the surface. And I'm not the only one who notices. Women sometimes forget that men are attracted to their energy, their ability to reach toward happiness and let it flow through them, not what's on the outside." Eli pressed his cheek against her hair for a moment, just steeping himself in the scent and feel of her. He felt his senses becoming intoxicated. "What's that delicious smell?"

Nestled within the warmth of his embrace, she felt as if she danced inside a dream. "*Lavender* soap. Handmade by Aunt Miriam. She is a woman of many talents."

Eli chuckled and then kissed the scarf protecting her hair so she couldn't really feel it. But he could. "She is indeed. And I'm so glad that one of her talents is baking. And canning."

Ripples of pleasure undulated through Eli. He could feel Sarah's breath caress the skin of his neck. "You should taste her double chocolate layer cake. She makes one for everyone's birthday. I confess. I spilled the beans."

He could taste it, feel it, every time she exhaled. Or was that simply him being intoxicated by her? Eli wasn't sure, but was more than willing to carry out experiments to find out. He inhaled again and let the sensation wash over his body in waves.

She was slightly tipsy with her exuberance, and all the more adorable for it. "What did you tell her, Sarah?"

"I might have told her when your birthday is so she can prepare in advance," Sarah said on a giggle. "And then she said she'd make you the chocolate layer cake with fudge frosting and a batch of oatmeal chocolate chip cookies to take home. She knows they are your favorite."

He pretended to be confused. "Could that possibly be because I eat an entire dozen every time she bakes them? How could she know? I was trying to be incognito."

Sarah punched him playfully on the shoulder. "Really, Eli? It's impossible for you to hide your out-of-control sweet tooth."

And maybe it was just the essence of her that filled his senses. Not chocolate or sugar. Maybe it was just the smell of her skin, of her hair. Of *her*, that was making him crazy and drawing him each and every day to her *haus* just to take another shot of Sarah Martin as if he were drinking moonshine straight from the earthenware jug.

He held her closer as they danced.

Chapter 22

The trip back to her *haus* seemed to end before it had begun. Due to her exhaustion, Sarah had just sat back, leaning against the cushioned bench seat, her eyes slipping closed, only to snap them open again. It was time to get out. Aunt Miriam had left a lamp lit in the picture window overlooking the front porch.

She tried not to be too obvious as she stretched, getting the kinks out of her shoulders. She turned to Eli who was back in his suspenders, shirt and pants. They'd changed before leaving the Ribeye and *nee* one had noticed when they'd left the restrooms sans their black masks. "Now, aren't you glad I made you go? It was the most fun I've had in a long time. Not since we were *kinner*."

He pretended to hold onto the lie, knowing she knew better. But she saw right through him because his eyes twinkled with teasing. "*Nee.*"

"Your nose is growing." She touched it as she made the announcement, leaning over in the seat, the strings of her *kapp* dangling between them.

This had to be some kind of a celestial test and if she wasn't careful, she'd fail it.

"All right, just call me Pinocchio then." Getting out, he rounded the horse to hitch it and help her down from the buggy. She clasped her palm in his warm one, feeling the electricity travel between them. "I'm glad you made me go. Now, my nose has returned to its normal size. But it was only a *gut* time because you were there."

"I'm glad." Sarah allowed him to help her out even though she was perfectly capable of jumping down on her own. It was the perfect excuse to touch him again. Something she couldn't get enough of. "Perfect thing to say." She rose to her feet, then remained where she stood for a second. "Especially to a woman who is having trouble feeling her legs."

"Did we dance too much?" he asked.

She shook her head. "I have discovered since you returned, Eli Troyer, that a woman can never dance too much. But on the subject of too much, I think maybe I did have too much soda. Coca-Cola from the soda fountain is my vice and all the sugar has gone to my head. My heart is pounding most rapidly."

But that's because of you. And your touch. And yet... I will deny it.

Surprised, he looked at her incredulously. "Two glasses over the course of an entire evening is hardly too much sugar. You eat more than that when you indulge in Miriam's latest baked drug."

She laughed at his joke. Miriam's baked goods were so addictive they probably were much like a drug of the *Englisch* world. She pointed toward the front porch and the legion of steps that seemed to have erected in her absence. Were there only five? Why, it seemed like twenty and she struggled to get her legs to move. "Then why did the stairs suddenly get steeper and taller?"

He looked at the stairs in question and laughed, playing along. "Maybe it's the lighting. Or lack thereof." Then, in the spirit of the evening and the costume he'd just removed only thirty minutes ago, he went with an impulse. "But I tell you what, there's a perfectly simple solution to this navigation problem you seem to think you have."

"Oh?" She raised her eyes to look at him, trying to keep the pounding of her heart at a minimum. "What?"

"This."

The next moment, Sarah found herself scooped up in his arms. A thrill ricocheted through her before she thought to protest. "Wait, you'll hurt your back."

He mustered a wounded look. "Are you trying to insult my manhood? I lift furniture ten times your weight every day. You weigh about the same as a headboard."

"Never," she breathed. Settling in, she twined her arms around his neck and sighed contentment as he carried her up the porch steps.

"*Gut*, because a grade school, out of shape lad could carry you up the stairs, Sarah," he said, not even shifting her weight, carrying her as if she were indeed, weightless.

"You must have a lot of headboards in the shop," she murmured, her breath warm against his chest as she rested her head there.

She closed her eyes, enjoying the sweet sensation of him carrying her up the stairs to the front door. Imagining they'd just left the church after having been joined together in the sanctity of marriage. Enjoying the rhythmic beating of her heart. Of his. With a sigh, she waited for him to set her down.

When he didn't, she opened her eyes to look at him.

"What?" she whispered, not wanting to do anything to break the spell but compelled to know the answer.

She wanted him to continue holding her. Carrying her. She wanted to be able to lay down her burdens at his feet and know that he'd be there for her. That he wouldn't leave her again.

"Just thinking," he said.

He sounded so serious.

"About what?" she repeated.

"Things I shouldn't be."

"Maybe you shouldn't be *thinking* them," she told him quietly as he set her down and her feet touched the porch. Feeling oddly confident, she turned the knob. "Maybe you should be *doing* something about them instead."

"You don't know what you're saying, Sarah." Opening the door, he stood back to let her enter first.

"I think I do." She walked into the foyer. There was only the one lamp on, casting a dim pool of light on the hardwood floors. Her heart began to pound. "I haven't had that much soda, if that's what you're thinking."

When he looked at her like that, she felt herself sinking into his eyes. "What I'm thinking is that I want you, Sarah. And I shouldn't."

"Why?" The word hung in the air between them as she turned her face up to his. "Is wanting me such a terrible thing?"

"*Jah.*" He visibly struggled. Shoulders tense, brow furrowed. Losing the fight with honor, with decency. "*Nee.*"

She swallowed, silently willing him to ask her. To ask her to be his *frau*. To say the words aloud and put an end to the ache in her soul. "Which is it?"

"Depends on who you are," he told her softly, his fingers reached out to twirl the string of her *kapp*. "Me. Or you."

"Me, Sarah," she told him, her voice hardly above an inviting whisper. "The same Sarah you've known for many years. And for me, having you want me isn't a terrible thing." She drew the only conclusion she could and prayed he'd tell her that she was wrong. "That means it must be a terrible thing for you, Eli, and I wonder why."

"Sarah, this isn't some kind of a twisted game," he said, scrubbing one trembling hand down his face. "This is our lives we're talking about. Our whole lives."

She'd never believed that, not for a moment. The stakes were far too high for it to be a game to her. Her eyes searched his face for a clue as to what he was thinking. "But there will be steps forward and backward, won't there?"

"Yes." Eli framed her face, wanting her more than he wanted to wake up the next morning. "There will be gains and losses. And I don't want to lose. Not anything."

She'd be affected, too. But not if he kissed her right now in the foyer. Not if she could, just once, feel that he was hers. She had been his for far too long without the brand. Now, she wanted it. All of it.

"Prove it, Eli," she whispered, her lips a fraction away from his.

He surrendered. "Sarah, you don't know what you're asking."

"*Jah*, I do."

Rising up on her toes, Sarah ended the internal debate for him by sealing her mouth to his.

The instant she did, Eli pulled her urgently into his arms, unleashing the wild, erotic emotions that had been beating their wings so wildly within her. For years. And years.

And years.

***

More than anything in the world, he wanted to completely claim her, to take her and make her his once and for all. The way he'd already done so many times in his mind it was like a loop playing on repeat. Since before the days when Levi had laid any claim to her. Since before the days when he knew he couldn't take her this way.

But tonight, there was something about her, about the uninhibited look in her eyes. Something about the feel of her body as she'd held it against his while they were dancing. Something about her.

His Sarah. The only one for him.

Eli was helpless to fight off the urgent demands of his own body when faced with a warm, open invitation from hers. Standing in the darkened foyer, he felt himself getting lost in the taste of her mouth, the sweetness of her breath, the softness of her curves as they molded against him.

He kissed her over and over again, his blood rushing, his mind swimming. He caressed the curve of her back and the slope of her shoulder, fighting to keep from touching the bare skin of her neck. But oh, he wanted to. To feel that silken skin under his fingers as her pulse throbbed its yearning underneath his hand. He wanted tonight to be memorable for her, not something to be filed away under the regret tab as a result of unchecked passion that had gotten out of hand. Above all, he wanted to make her happy and eradicate any thought of Levi from her mind and body forever.

The sound of crying pierced the disjointed thoughts racing through his mind.

Gasping for air, Sarah drew her head back. How could they have forgotten? "The twins."

They weren't alone.

The realization of what he'd almost let himself do penetrated Eli's consciousness. It was his responsibility to keep Sarah safe. Even if that meant keeping her safe from *him*. But here he was in Miriam's entryway, unable to stay the raging desire within his traitorous body.

Even after they'd pulled apart and a foot of space lay between them, his body still throbbed and hummed. Missing her and feeling her loss. He'd completely forgotten himself. Completely forgotten his obligations and had been a heartbeat away from giving into needs that had been his daily companions for as long as he could remember.

Longer.

"I – I'd better tell Miriam she's off the clock for the midnight feeding," Sarah stammered. "It's the least I can do after she let me go on this merry journey tonight and indulge my costume fantasy."

"Speaking of going, I guess I should be doing the same," Eli murmured, not able to hide his shame over his actions.

Why was it, when he was with this woman, he forgot every ounce of his integrity? *Gott's* path was clear and it was never acceptable to take advantage of a single woman, even if she offered herself. Why did he constantly put himself into situations with her that made him yearn to turn his back on every value he knew he couldn't in *gut* conscience forsake?

Unable to answer his own questions, a red-faced Eli began to cross to the door. It shouldn't end like this, on such an awkward note. Not when the night had been one of the best of his life. He didn't want her to think he was rejecting her or what had almost happened between them. What he was rejecting was his own bad behavior. As the man, he needed to be the leader of the relationship and he'd failed her again.

Her hand on the banister, Sarah paused. "Can I interest you in a cup of coffee while I feed the *bopplis*?"

She could interest him in a great many things, coffee only being at the end of the long list. He shook his head. Eli found he was in far deeper than he ever imagined he would be. Resisting Sarah was becoming increasingly more difficult each time he was faced with the temptation.

Because being with her felt so right.

This time the twins had come to his rescue like two tiny white knights mounted on their chargers of high-pitched cries. The next time, there may not be a wake-up call coming to the aid of his lax conscience at the eleventh hour. The next time, he might give in and do something completely inappropriate that they would both regret later. Something that would bring shame upon them both in the eyes of their community.

And he'd become hopelessly caught in a tender, tempting trap he had absolutely *nee* business being in. One where the only escape would be to gnaw off his own leg. Eli sighed inwardly. Once he was with Sarah, it seemed hopeless to do the right thing. And it was almost humanly impossible to keep her at arm's length. And to rectify that situation, he needed to cease his daily visits.

"Coffee sounds great, but it will keep me awake and it's getting late," he said, opening the door. "I've got to be at the shop early tomorrow morning. That dining table needs to be finished for delivery on Monday."

She sighed. "You're working on Sunday? I know there's *nee* church tomorrow, but shouldn't you be resting on the holy day? You work too hard, Eli."

It was a lie that she saw right through, tempting her to compare him to his *dat* with her passive aggressive comment but it was the best he could do with his brain scrambled this way. He wasn't accustomed to lying, especially not to her. But the alternative was to stay, and he couldn't do that either.

"*Gut* evening, Sarah."

Chapter 23

The woman never saw the man coming.

So preoccupied with her hurricane of worry, her vapid eyes never saw him until she felt him. One minute she was making her way to the bakery on the other side of the narrow street, to find out the directions to Sarah Martin's *haus*. The next minute, the criminal hurtled his muscular body right at her.

A scream echoed in her throat as he pummeled into her. The knees that used to support her wavered. Swayed. Until she fell backward, pin wheeling, flailing, falling.

A solid mountain of a man without a face.

Something black was wrapped around his head, obscuring his features from her vision. She thought she saw two sinister eyes boring into her, but she couldn't be sure. It might have just been the sudden flare of white hot panic burning her lungs. And then the growing pain in her head blotted out everything before that also faded away.

"Can you hear me?" a soothing voice asked.

She felt someone patting her hand, and she struggled to open her eyes. When she did, she found herself looking up into the face of a woman she'd never seen before. An older woman with short gray hair and a wrinkled, concerned smile that shone now with relief. The woman's eyes, bright and alert, seemed to be searching her face for something. But what? She didn't even know this woman. Or did she? Oh, her head pounded with such violent intensity she couldn't hold rational thought.

"Are you all right, hon?"

Holding tightly to the woman's hand, she raised herself up. The immediate world refused to come into focus, spinning around her. She had to get to Sarah Martin and of that she was certain. To tell the other woman what she knew.

"I don't know?" she answered hoarsely. Fear and confusion fought a dual with tiny, pointy straight pens, sticking her as she tried to pull her thoughts together.

And found that there weren't any more thoughts to pull.

Panic superseded pain.

Eyes widening, she stared at the woman. Her voice shook when she asked, "Where am I?"

"This is Pride, hon," the woman told her kindly. "And some horrible creature smacked you over your head to steal the overnight satchel you were carrying. I saw the whole thing," she volunteered, then added with a note of frustration, "but I couldn't stop him." She shook her head. "I don't even know who he was; he was wearing some kind of a stocking over his head like in those movies about bank robbers. Some Clint Eastwood wanna be." The older woman shook her head again, lamenting. "Nothing like this has ever happened in Pride before. This community has a lot of Amish and there isn't any crime in their community. Are you Amish, dear?"

"Pride?" she echoed, trying to sneak words past the excruciating pain in her head. "Do you know Sarah Martin?"

The name of the town meant nothing to her. The only thing that floated across her consciousness was the name Sarah Martin. She racked her brain to try and figure out why she needed to talk to Sarah but her head just hurt too much so she clamped her eyes shut against it. The details the other woman had just recited did nothing but confuse her further. She didn't remember anyone hitting her or taking something from her.

She couldn't remember anything. Except Sarah. She needed to get to Sarah. For something very important.

"Yes, Pride," the other woman repeated patiently. "Pride, Ohio, the most peaceful city I've ever had the pleasure of living in. And my dad was a United States Marine so I lived in ten places before I graduated from high school." She beamed for a moment but then the smile faded as she bent closer to look her over. "I live a couple of blocks away and was just out for my evening walk," she explained. "Why don't I take you home, make you a nice cup of hot tea while we call for Sheriff Kent? Unless you have a reservation at the bed-and-breakfast over there." She nodded vaguely over her shoulder at the street just beyond.

"No, I don't have a reservation," she answered hoarsely. At least, she didn't think she had one. She didn't know.

"Do you think you can walk, Emma?"

She looked up sharply at the woman. Did they know one another? Was the woman someone to her? "Why did you call me Emma?"

Looking perplexed, the woman touched something at the base of her throat. A moment later, the sensation registered. Metal. She was wearing a gold chain with a cross dangling from it. Engraved underneath, was the name of a *boppli*. Named after her. That, she remembered.

"That's what it says engraved right there." The older woman read the word and then raised her eyes to Emma's face. "That's your name, isn't it?"

The young woman looked at her blankly. "I think so."

Chapter 24

"I do declare, I haven't seen such a spate of excitement in this town since, I don't even remember." Bustling into Eli's wood shop, Miriam flung her hands in the air to gain his attention so he'd shut off the lathe. He gestured her to the small office and offered her a wooden chair. "I brought you these." She took a small plate of oatmeal chocolate chip cookies out of her bag and placed them on his desk. "Still a little warm," she said proudly. "I know how much you like them. A full dozen."

Eli felt himself about to be steamrolled. This was the first time he'd seen Miriam since the night of the costume party and that devastating kiss with Sarah. He'd made his decision on the way home that night. He'd been going to Miriam's *haus* too much and that had to stop for all their sakes. Before the situation passed the point of *nee* return.

Nee one could've been more surprised at Miriam's sudden appearance in his furniture shop, requesting a private moment, than he was. He wondered if it had to do with Sarah. His heart started to pound. There couldn't be anything wrong, could there? With Sarah or the *bopplis*?

He looked at the plate. "You really shouldn't have gone to the trouble."

"*Nee* trouble at all. I like baking. I like knowing what's going on, too," she added craftily. "Which is why I'd hate to be Bishop Beiler right now. That man is so busy, trying to find the twins' rightful parents and now he's got to deal with the other Emma." Not standing on ceremony, she reached over and peeled back the covering on the plate she'd brought, taking a cookie for herself. "He stopped by the *haus* last night. Seems the victim in the mugging is named Emma and she kept asking after Sarah Martin."

"Why on earth would a stranger on the street be asking after Sarah?" Eli asked with a gasp.

"Bishop Beiler is wondering the same thing," Miriam said. "The woman's memory is coming back in bits and pieces and all we know right now is that her name is Emma and she's looking for Sarah Martin. She didn't have any papers or anything that revealed her full identity. She's Amish. Although she wasn't dressed as such the day she was attacked. It's all very perplexing."

"Emma?" Eli asked, thinking so hard he felt like his head might explode. "The *boppli's* name is Emma? Do you think she's related?"

"She thinks she is, but this Emma has never had any *kinner*." Miriam clucked her tongue. "They were able to ascertain that fact at the hospital. She's not our Emma's *mamm*."

Eli was surprised Miriam was his first visitor in regards to this revelation. It was hard to live in Pride and escape the local gossip making the rounds. The day after the mugging had happened, Emma's information had to have spread like wildfire through town. Especially, since it had happened right out in the street.

"She gave them a description?" Eli pointed out. "The *Englisch* witness?"

Miriam snorted. "Some description. A medium-sized, muscled man with a nylon stocking on his head. If the streetlight hadn't highlighted a tattoo of a wolf on his forearm, there would've been nothing to set him apart from scores of other two-bit thugs. But those types never stay in Pride. If we have to worry about crime now, I'm not sure I feel safe going into town. I'm not a spring chicken anymore. *Nee* telling what might happen."

Eli took a bite of one of Miriam's offerings and felt himself softening to the invasion. He couldn't resist the cookies and allowed the sweet confection to melt across his tongue before speaking again. "Not too many men running around Pride with stockings pulled over their faces," he quipped. "We don't even have stockings here in our small community." And then he leaned back in his chair and studied Miriam's face. "But you didn't come just to talk to me about this mysterious other Emma. What's the real reason you came here, Miriam?"

Miriam purposely avoided his eyes. "I wanted to ask your advice about something."

He was aware that she had several so he played along. "I can't imagine you needing my advice about much of anything."

Miriam waved her hand vaguely in the air. "I do." And then she looked at him, leaning closer over the desk. "It's more about *someone*, Eli." She took a deep breath. "I know someone with a malady. Her heart. It's broken. Like that ornate scrolled table leg I saw laying on the floor out in the shop. Shattered into pieces."

He paused, treading carefully. "I'm not sure I can use wood glue to put a heart back together."

Miriam frowned. "It's not that kind of break."

For a talkative woman, Miriam certainly did take a long time getting to the point. "Oh?"

Proceeding cautiously, Miriam nodded. "*Someone* has broken it."

Jah, Levi. I already tried to put it back together. I failed.

"This someone. She told you this?"

Miriam shrugged vaguely. "Some things, you just know. Anyway, she's in love with this really wonderful young man, but for some reason, they just can't seem to get together." She looked at him pointedly. "I don't think he's getting the message."

"Sounds like an imbecile," he said, evading. Knowing it wouldn't work with the ever sharp and stubborn Miriam. "Maybe he doesn't have feelings for her."

He has feelings for her. In fact, he loves her.

"Oh, he has feelings," Miriam assured him firmly. "But he's hiding them. The fact of the matter is, he didn't have the greatest relationship with his own family. Not with his *vader* and I don't think he thinks he knows how to have a true and loving relationship with a *frau*. Meanwhile, she – my *wunderbarr* someone," Miriam emphasized, "– is just pining away in silence." Her eyes pinned him. "What can I do to help these fools?"

Eli was dumbfounded that Miriam had taken it upon herself to act like some kind of elderly matchmaker. He sincerely doubted that Sarah had put her up to this. Sarah would probably be mortified if she knew.

"Nothing," he told her firmly, returning her look. "There is nothing you can do. You might not have all the facts at your disposal."

Miriam wouldn't allow him to evade. To run like the scared idiot he knew he was.

"Oh, I think I do," she pressed.

"No," he countered, his eyes holding hers, "you don't."

She continued with the charade though she must know that they were both talking about Sarah. "I know this *vader* was *nee gut*, just like Levi's *vader*. My own *bruder*. But that doesn't mean anything. Trouble is, he seems to think it does. There's *nee* other reason for him to be holding back. He's *nothing* like his *dat*."

That she was right on target astounded him. Except for everything but him being like his *dat*. Of that, he wasn't quite sure. The subject was painful and he didn't want to talk about it. Eli was perfectly aware that his *vader's* icy temperament was not a secret in Pride, but that still didn't make the memory any easier to deal with. There was also Levi to consider and his friend's *vader*, too. Both issues made it hard for Eli to contemplate a life with Sarah. He'd already failed one *frau*. It would break his heart into thousands of muscled shards if he destroyed Sarah's life, too.

With a terse movement, he put the top back on the plate of cookies, silently turning down the offering. "Could be he's right to hold back. Maybe he cares about this person so much he's willing to sacrifice everything to protect her. Keep her safe."

Miriam frowned. "If that were the case, then every child of every criminal would be a criminal. Like the stocking-faced man. You don't believe that, do you?"

She was twisting things. "That's different."

"Only if you make yourself believe that." Miriam shook her head. "I'm not talking about just any someone."

Eli sighed. "I didn't think so."

"Sarah's in love with you. She's never said a word, but I can tell." Miriam leveled her gaze at him. "And you're in love with her."

His patience worn thin, Eli rose from his seat. He turned toward the older woman. "Miriam, I don't have time to argue about this or tell you how wrong you are. I've got a customer coming in a few minutes to pick up their table. And I want to polish it before they get here. So it shines."

Unlike the darkness that has settled in my soul.

"You can argue all you want. It still doesn't change anything. About either one of you," Miriam said. "Sarah's finally right in front of you. Close enough to touch. Don't look away, Eli Troyer. If you do, you'll miss her. Your perfect match."

Eli just nodded. He'd say or do anything to get Miriam to leave and end this uncomfortable discussion.

Then, with her head held high, Miriam crossed to the door. "All right, I said my peace. The next step is up to you. It better be the right one. Don't let Levi and Vernon's deaths be for nothing. There's been too much death and sorrow and not enough light. Something *gut* can come of it. But only if you let it."

And with that, she slipped out of the office, leaving him staring at the open doorway.

Eli scrubbed his hand over his face. It was worse than he thought, and he was going to have to do something about it.

Chapter 25

"She's their aunt, Sarah," Bishop Beiler explained. "And since their *mamm* passed, she and her family have come to collect them. They'll have a *gut* home. With their family. This aunt isn't able to have *kinner* of her own and *boppli* Emma is her namesake."

Even though the bishop's words made perfect sense, Sarah didn't want to accept them. Miriam, Sarah and Bishop Beiler sat at the dining room table. Sarah sat in silence with her head bowed and her hands grasping furiously at her skirt. She couldn't sit still. Just couldn't accept that her twins were leaving after all these months. Going home. She'd become so attached to them. And Eli wasn't here. He didn't even care.

Emma Yoder had finally gotten her entire memory back and remembered why she'd wanted to visit Sarah Martin. Her sister, Rebecca, had been afflicted with post-partum depression so severe she'd taken her own life. The twins were now orphans because their *dat* had been killed in a farming accident almost right after their birth. Between the hormone fluctuations, lack of help in the *haus* and the grief over her *mann's* untimely demise, Rebecca had dropped the *bopplis* off at Sarah's.

Word had traveled to Rebecca's community, just one county over, about the tragic loss of Levi and Vernon. That had planted the seed in

Rebecca's head that she could gain some relief if she gave them away to a *mamm* who had tragically lost her own infant. Rebecca had known that Sarah Martin would take care of her twins. In a twisted way, Rebecca wanted to help Sarah. Ease her pain. Not thinking clearly, she'd abandoned the *bopplis* on the porch and then deliberately driven her buggy into an oncoming grain truck on her way back home.

"I know it's a lot to take in, Sarah," Bishop Beiler said in a soothing tone.

"When is this Emma coming to get the twins?" Sarah asked in a shaky voice. Miriam placed her palm over Sarah's in comfort.

"Tomorrow."

Sarah hissed in a ragged breath. "So soon? I haven't had time to get use to the idea. I haven't had a chance to say goodbye. He's not ..."

The bishop's head snapped up. "Who's not?"

Miriam watched Sarah and the tears pooling in her eyes. Eli hadn't returned since the night of the costume party and she hadn't seen him at all. What she'd kept hidden was how much she missed him.

"Bishop," the older woman said, "I think what Sarah's trying to say is that Samuel's just started walking and he's not ready to leave yet. But we'll get through this. We understand that this Emma is next of kin to the twins."

The devastation on Sarah's face was palpable and cast a pall of gloom over the room. Miriam stroked Sarah's hand. Katie bustled about getting the bishop a cup of coffee. The sounds reverberated through Sarah's ears like cannon fire even though they were at low volume. She'd lost Eli. Again. Now, she was losing her *bopplis*. *Nee*. Not her *bopplis*. But they'd wormed their way into her heart just the same.

"I'll be going now, Sarah," Bishop Beiler said as he stood. "Emma and I will be by tomorrow afternoon to collect the twins. Can you have them ready? I trust we won't need Sheriff Kent's assistance?"

Sarah couldn't speak or she'd collapse into a puddle of tears and sobs so she just gave a slight nod of her head. Didn't even make eye contact with the older man.

She'd tried to be strong, she really had. When she'd seen Bishop Beiler at the door, her stomach had fallen to her feet. Because deep in her heart, she'd already known that the *bopplis* were leaving. Sarah had gone through an entire gamut of feelings: agony, anger, despair, and then endured them in reverse order. All without hearing a word from Eli. What she wouldn't give to gaze upon his face and have her say that everything would work out. He'd been absent again in her time of need. Didn't he know how much his solid presence would help her in this situation?

The stillness and impending doom made her edgy. By the end of the day, Sarah figured she'd lasted as long as she could. Asking Miriam to stay with the twins and without giving away her feelings or thoughts, Sarah walked over to Eli's wood shop and stood outside the door. She could hear the whir of the generator. Should she knock? Just walk in? She'd decided this was a very bad idea and had turned to leave when the lathe went silent. She turned back around and opened the door a crack.

"Who is it?" His deep, strong voice washed over her in waves. She hadn't realized truly how much she'd missed him until this moment.

"Eli?" she called, voice shaking with emotion.

"Sarah?" he said, then she saw him.

He stepped away from the machine and stood underneath a ray of sunlight shining down from a crack in the ceiling. Lit from above, he resembled an angel. Her angel. *Nee.* Not anymore, she thought with a shake of her head. He was not to be counted upon.

"Jah."

"Sarah, what are you doing here in the middle of the day?" he asked.

She reared back and considered leaving. He didn't want her here.

He didn't want *her*.

"The *bopplis*," she repeated, struggling to keep the panic and pain she felt from overtaking her vocal chords.

"Sarah, you're scaring me," he said, striding closer to stand right in front of her. But he kept his hands at his sides when she needed the comfort of physical touch more than any other time in her life. Even when she'd lost Vernon. She'd been stronger then because she'd only lost three people she loved. Now, she was about to lose three more. And it felt like everything. "What is wrong with the *bopplis*? Do you need help? Should I follow you home?"

"*Nee*," she said with a shake of her head. Tears pricked the back of her eyes again and it seemed all she wanted to do today was cry. But not in front of him. "They're leaving. Tomorrow."

Even though she knew she was being cryptic and his stiff body posture indicated his frustration at her lack of reasonable explanation, she couldn't push anymore words past the lump in her throat.

Eli made an assumption. "So, their *mamm* has been found then. How do we know she won't do something like this again? That the *bopplis* are safe with her?"

Sarah stood there for long, tense moments that dragged on. The generator still hummed in the background. Birds chirped outside the paned window. The sun streamed in from outside. Eli stood solid and concerned in front of her. But he didn't touch her. Didn't reach out. And time stood still.

"She's dead."

He took a step back, widening the gap when she wanted to close it. "What?"

Sarah's hands fluttered up toward her chest. And then she made a fatal mistake. She locked eyes with him. One lonely tear escaped her eyelid and waterfalled down her flushed cheek. Then another. And another. Until she couldn't stop them. Her face was awash with her pain.

Eli finally crossed the space between them and placed both hands along the sides of her jaw.

Then he pulled her in close to his chest and simply held her there. Strong. Unyielding. So much time passed that Sarah lost track of it. The great heaving sobs racked her body until she couldn't even stand on her own power. Eli held her upright. Without much awareness of what was happening, Sarah felt him lift her up and cradle her in his arms while he strode toward his office. He placed her gently down in the padded chair in the corner and handed her a handkerchief.

She heaved another breath and looked into his eyes. Nothing but concern reflected back to her.

"Why don't you start at the beginning?" he asked in a soft tone.

She nodded and took another fortifying breath. "Bishop Beiler stopped by earlier and right away, I knew. Did you hear about that woman who was robbed last week right in front of the bakery?"

Eli nodded and crouched down beside her so they were more eye level. "I did."

"Well, it turns out, she was coming to find me. Her sister, Rebecca, is the *bopplis' mamm*. She had some severe depression after their birth. She killed herself soon after she left them on my doorstep. Close to her home. They didn't find a note until they went through her things months later. Her sister, Emma, is that woman. And she's come for them, Eli. She can't have any *kinner* and she wants *my* twins!"

Too late, Sarah realized what she had revealed and clamped a hand over her mouth as if she could push the words back inside it.

Eli reached out to run a soothing hand up and down her arm. "I know what you mean, Sarah. You've had them so long, cared for them, loved them, that you feel as if they are now a part of you. I don't think anyone would begrudge you these feelings. Not even this other Emma."

She sat in silence. Now, that the words were out and he hadn't rejected her, some of the oppressive weight had been lifted from her mood. A flicker of irritation penetrated.

"Why haven't I seen you since the night we went to the costume party?"

He plunked his rear down on the hardwood floor and sighed. "I thought it would be best for us to have some space. And Miriam."

Sarah scrunched her face up into a grimace. "Miriam? What does she have to do with any of it?"

Eli narrowed his eyes. "She paid me an unexpected visit last week."

"Why would she do that?" Sarah asked, but she suspected she already knew the answer. Miriam meant well but meddling was her specialty.

"She thinks we belong together. That we're more than friends." His eyes searched hers.

***

All Eli wanted was a sign. Her eyes, as wide as saucers, stared at him but didn't really see him. Like she looked right through him. But then, the emotional turmoil she'd endured could have set Sarah to unraveling.

"Miriam shouldn't have come," she whispered. "She should mind her own business. What does she know about me or my life? What's best for it?"

Eli knew he needed to tread carefully, lest the entire situation blow up in his face. Her distress over the *bopplis* leaving, coupled with her infernal pride made for an explosive emotional cocktail.

"I think Miriam just wants what's best for you. She wants you to be happy."

Sarah snorted. "She wants to control me. And stick her nose in where it doesn't belong. She doesn't know what I went through with Levi. None of it."

Eli paused to let those words sink in. "I think she knows more than you think. Or more than she's letting on right now. It was common knowledge that John Martin was a mean and violent man. The apple rarely falls that far from the tree. I'm just angry with myself that I didn't see it. Until it was too late."

Sarah was quick to come to his defense. "How would you know, Eli? I didn't know either. He showed absolutely *nee* tendencies. There were *nee* warning signs that would lead either of us to believe that he'd turn out like his *dat*. That he didn't have the strength to break the cycle."

Eli wasn't certain he deserved Sarah serving as his champion. "*Nee*. I should have known it just by the very nature and cycle of abuse. It's difficult to end the vicious circle."

"Levi's behavior was all my fault."

How could she say that? How could she possibly even think that? "*Nee*. It wasn't. Any more than it was my fault for ever allowing you to marry him. Levi knew better. He was responsible for his own actions." Allowing himself a more intimate contact, he reached for her hand, but she pulled it away. "Trust me, Sarah."

She shook her head, her voice hollow. "I doubt if I can. Ever again. I was beginning to, but now that's gone." Her eyes were accusing. "Just like you'll be."

Why was she making this so hard for him? Didn't she know how he felt about her? How he'd always felt? "Didn't you hear me? You're not responsible for any of this. And I'm not going to leave Pride."

She pulled herself into a ball and hugged herself as if she could protect her body from the pain. "It's not about you leaving Pride, Eli. It's about you leaving *me*. You're still supposed to be my friend. Where were you this week when I needed you?"

He was insulting her with a lie. Because he did love her, and he didn't want to be separated from her. Not even for one second. Sarah fisted her hands in her lap. "Please, spare me that platitude. Spare me that at least." Her voice took on a martyr-like quality as she rolled her eyes heavenward. "If you cared about me, you would have been at my *haus* today when Bishop Beiler stepped over the threshold and shattered my heart."

His face was somber as he looked at her. "I would have been. It's..." If he could have taken that leap of faith for anyone, he would've taken it for her. Because he'd never loved anyone but her. But he was scared. The pain of losing one *frau* still too raw. He couldn't bear it if he lost Sarah, too. So tiny bits of her was infinitely better than none. He'd rather worship her from afar in safety than have the one tether of hope he still clung to snipped in two.

She strangled out a chuckle. "Words, Eli, just empty words."

Unable to remain calm any longer, Eli rose to his feet. "That's not fair! Why do you think it's easy for me, leaving you alone? Pretending like it doesn't kill me every time I walk away from you?"

"Well, it must be as easy to stomach as Aunt Miriam's famous cherry pie, because you're doing it," she shot back. "As fast as your long legs can carry you away."

Eli dug his knuckles into the skin of his knees as he leaned over, his face inches away from hers. "I'm doing it, woman, because if I continue to see you, I might do something rash. Even more rash than the things we've already done!"

She rose, too, facing him down. "Like what, Eli? Like love me? Marry me? Is that what you think is inappropriate?" Her eyes blazed fire. "Or are you afraid of suddenly feeling – what?" She thought of Levi, of why he'd gone out of his way to abuse and torment her. Because she'd disappointed him as a *frau* in every way. There wasn't any other explanation for it. She couldn't find fault in her personality. It had to be that. "Noble intentions mingled with yearning that you can't explain, causing this confliction? Is that why you're running away?"

"What are you talking about?" he asked.

"I'm talking about you running from me."

How much could he reveal without telling her everything? She had to be made to understand that the choice wasn't his to make. It had been preordained – if she were going to be happy. And above all, he wanted *her* to be happy.

"Don't you understand? I'm running from you because I can't stop thinking about you, because every time I see you, I want you. Because I want to make you my *frau*. I want everyone to know how much I care about you. I want to shout it to the heavens."

Sarah's frustration was palpable. He wasn't getting through to her. Reaching her.

"And this is what... repulsive to you?" Sarah fought back tears again. "You think you're insane for wanting me? For sharing a life? For allowing *Gott* to light our true path?"

Helpless, he took her hand and then dropped it between them as if they were both on fire. He began to pace the room. "I'm insane from wanting you. Don't you understand? I can't do that to you."

"Now I'm the one completely lost. Do what to me?" Sarah asked, confusion written over every line of her face.

Exasperation filled his voice. "Marry you."

She waited, but nothing more came in the wake of the declaration. "I'm still lost."

He said it is simply as he could. "I don't want to hurt you."

"And you think ignoring me is going to accomplish that?" she asked, hands flying through the air. "*Nee.* You ignoring me is what's hurtful."

Eli shook his head sadly. "*Jah.*" He had to stand firm in his belief about what was best for her. For him.

"Eli, what are you talking about?" Sarah asked in a voice laced with desperation. "You're not making any sense."

"I can't..." he said, shaking his head and sinking back down into a chair.

"Why would marrying you hurt me?" She wanted to stop pushing and let the words that remained float to the ground to be swallowed, unsaid. But that was impossible. Too much had been revealed. Too much space lay between them.

"Because," he said quietly, "I would hurt you in a way that would be worse than the stocking-faced man. Something even worse than Levi Martin."

She gasped and he welcomed the sound. The words were meant to scare her. Get her to back off and leave now. But instead, she pressed forward. "What? What could you possibly turn into that's worse than Levi? I've seen you at your worst, Eli. You don't frighten me with this ridiculous talk."

No, you haven't even come close to seeing me at my worst.

Turning away, he closed his eyes and gave her the rest of it. "I could become my *vader.*"

He could almost feel her blue eyes boring into his back, willing him to turn around. But he didn't want to. Didn't want to see the horror as it played across her face. When he didn't, she moved around him until she faced him. "Excuse me?"

"My *vader,*" he repeated. "Abel Troyer, a man who was dedicated to the constant quest of producing the most beautiful hand-crafted piece of furniture the world had ever seen, all the while breaking the heart of a woman whose feet he wasn't even fit to kiss. And his *kinner's*."

Chapter 26

Sarah remembered what Miriam had told her, but couldn't see the connection between *vader* and son, other than blood. They were nothing alike. Searching Eli's face, she saw that he seemed to believe otherwise. "You're serious. You're ignoring me in my time of need because you think you're going to turn into a cold man?" It didn't make sense to her. How could that be worse than violence?

"Not a cold man. My *vader*," he said shortly. "Although the two are synonymous."

How could he possibly believe what he was saying? Unless he was leading some double life she knew nothing about, and that simply wasn't possible in Pride, there was *nee* evidence for him to even begin to think he could be anything like his *vader*.

"*Ach*, Eli, is that why...?" She sank down in the chair, stunned by the revelation of what had been going on in his head all this time. "Is that what you think? That after a lifetime of being a *gut*, kind and decent human being, one who everyone admires, you are suddenly going to turn cold and allow ice to freeze around your heart?" It stole her breath away. The pieces began to fall together. "And here I thought..."

Eli looked at her. "You thought what?"

She blinked, attempting to reconcile things in her mind. "I thought that you pushed me toward Levi because you didn't want me."

He laughed at the absurdity of that. "I pushed you toward Levi not because I didn't want you, but I thought he could be everything for you that I couldn't be. For some warped reason, I thought he could love you more than I could. Because he had more to lose."

And that was the irony of it, she thought. "He did and he lost it all. He was mean, abusive and shallow as the river in March. Completely engaged in making rudeness his full-time hobby. Everything you weren't. Aren't."

True, the elder Troyer's blood ran thick in his veins. And now, finding out that Levi had turned into the elder Martin even though he'd tried in vain to fight it, well, that probably made Eli hold even tighter to his own fear until it wrapped around his heart like a vice. But she could peel the tentacles away with her love. "How can you be so sure?"

Pity filled her for what he had lived with. And anger for what he had made them both live with now. "Because I apparently know you a great deal better than you know yourself. Do you think this is genetic? Something that suddenly kicks in at a certain age?" She couldn't hold back the anger even though she tried. So many wasted years. So much misunderstanding. "Maybe there's a switch inside that just turns on after you say your vows before *Gott* and then you turn into a different person?"

His eyes told her she wasn't getting through, in spite of her best efforts at logic. Her frustration mounted. "Look at you, look at your life. Your *vader* was cold, always working, always frowning. You're selfless." She jabbed a finger into his chest right above his heart. "Right there, that's the proof. You are always thinking about others before yourself."

He shoved his hands into his pockets, looking away. "I was trying not to be like my *vader*."

"Are you about done?" Sarah stared at his back, which was so stiff, so formal. She felt him drifting away from her and there was nothing she could do. The frustration clawed at her, grasping and tearing at her chest cavity. "What makes you think that you can continue worrying about becoming your *vader* and not pay the ultimate price? It's *nee* way to live."

"The stakes are too high to risk finding out," he whispered, eyes vapid and empty.

"Why don't you leave that for *Gott* to decide?"

He shook his head, looking away, breaking eye contact. "I won't risk it."

Sarah looked at him in silence for long moments. The emptiness within her growing to astounding portions. Threatening to explode. She played her ace in the hole. "You might not be like your *vader*, but you're just like Levi. Neither one of you thought I was *gut* enough to love."

"That's not true." He reached for her, but she backed away, her eyes accusing.

"Isn't it?" she demanded, low and angry. She clamped her eyes shut, the blessed blackness behind her lids as dark as her soul felt. "Levi was always looking for something better, never giving me a chance to be that something better for him. And you, you're even worse. You won't even give it a chance at all before dismissing it out of turn."

"Nee."

Sarah pressed her lips together, fighting for control. Losing. "Well, it certainly isn't about love, is it? Because people who love each other try anything and everything they can to cherish what they have and more importantly, forge a future." Something tore within her. She'd had enough. "You know what? You can just hide here in your wood shop until you die of old age, I don't care anymore. I'm through caring. I'm never going to care about anyone ever again."

She crossed quickly to the door, then stopped, her hand on the knob. Sarah looked at him over her shoulder. "And I was wrong. You are like your *vader*. Not because you'd be a bad *mann* but because you're willing to hurt the people you love even when you know you shouldn't."

The door slammed in her wake.

***

The next few days were wrapped in a thick haze, moving around her, enveloping her in heavy and unwanted feelings. Sarah went through the motions, doing what was required of her, pushing ahead because it was the only thing that convinced her she was still alive, still breathing.

Bishop Beiler and Emma had come to collect the *bopplis* and she hadn't even cried. She just felt numb. Even though Samuel had wailed in sorrow when he'd been wrenched from her arms, she still hadn't broken down. Not even at night alone in her cold bed.

It amazed her how long a person could keep moving after their heart had been reduced to shattered pieces.

Aunt Miriam and Katie noticed and tried their best not to appear as if they had. It was impossible not to detect that the spirit had left her voice and the passion had left her eyes. But she was trying. Trying very hard. She had to admit that Emma was a lovely woman and she'd take wonderful care of the *bopplis*, her own niece and nephew. Her tear-filled eyes had shone brightly with love for them. And now, they'd be as dear to her as her own *kinner* could have been.

But the logical facts of the situation didn't even begin to ease the pervasive ache that swathed Sarah. And for their parts, Miriam, Katie, and Suzanne were incredibly careful, mentioning *nee* topics heavier than the selection of Miriam's latest baked good. She blessed them for it. Blessed them for not asking, not trying to help a situation that was beyond mending.

The only thing that would do any *gut* was time. And she would have plenty of that. Alone, she mused as she stood in the attic, finally going through the trunks she'd been avoiding. Now, the mindless task got her through the day.

"Don't get mixed up with handsome men," she said to the bumblebee that had flown in through the vents to join her. "Or any men for that matter. It's not worth the hassle."

"You're right."

Startled, she looked up and saw Eli standing in the doorway. Something pulled within her stomach, tight and hard. He hadn't been by, on any pretext, for the last few days. She'd pretended it didn't matter. Acted nonchalant to prepare herself for the times she wouldn't be able to avoid running into him.

He's come to see about the bopplis. Because he never came to say goodbye.

Closing the trunk, she picked up an old dress and tried to act as if her heart wasn't about to beat right out of her chest. "Right about which part?"

Circles shadowed his eyes. He hadn't been sleeping. That made two of them.

Like a man testing icy waters, he slowly entered the room. "Take your pick."

"They're both accurate statements."

She tried to get a better view of his face, to read his expression. Not sure why he'd now all of a sudden decided to come. What he was after. "*Ach*, I hope not. I was just being facetious."

"I know."

"Why are you here today?" With effort, she kept her voice efficiently without emotion. "Is there something you need?"

"I hear Katie went back home."

"*Jah*," Sarah answered. "Jacob came to fetch her. Said he couldn't live without her and their *boppli*. He made amends for his callousness."

Like you should.

Getting down on his knees beside her, he started picking up some old dishes, placing them back into the one trunk still open. "*Jah*. I know the feeling."

She froze and looked at him. "That's a string of words, Eli. What do they mean?"

His eyes met hers. Searching. Her heart remained closed, devoid of the hope that usually lingered there. Maybe he was too late. "Depends."

"On what?"

Tossing the spoon he held aside, Eli took her hands in his and slowly rose to his feet, bringing her up with him. "On whether I can get you to forgive me."

"About which part? I can think of a lot of things that could be applicable to you begging for forgiveness."

He didn't take a breath, just plunged in. "All of it. I've been ignorant..."

The smile flirted with her lips and then spread into an easy grin as she nodded. "Go on. So far, I'm in agreement. Definitely ignorant."

"I've been running scared of my *dat's* shadow for so long, I was doing exactly the very thing I didn't want to do," he pleaded, squeezing her hands. "I was hurting you. I sent you into Levi's arms and let him hurt you, too."

The anger in her heart fled. Chased away on a beam of light as if it had never been there. "It's not as if you could see into the future."

She'd always been quick to forgive, but maybe, he wasn't. Not when it came to himself. "No, but maybe if I had a little more faith in the man I could be..."

Her smile widened and she released the breath she'd been holding. "As if you didn't know, I had faith enough for the two of us."

"Had." He emphasized the single word that could wound him. Not understanding her. "Does that mean...?"

Because her heart was moved, she rose and kissed his cheek.

His next words came out in a tumble. "Would you be willing to marry me?"

Her mouth dropped open, but she snapped it shut. "There's only one way to know for certain."

His eyes searched hers and she smiled. It felt like coming home. "And that is?"

Sarah's insides felt like butterflies flitting through a spring meadow. "Ask me."

Taking her hands in his again, he looked into her eyes. "Sarah, will you make me the happiest man on *Gott's* earth and consent to become my *frau*?"

She pulled them away, placing one over her pounding heart. She fluttered her lashes and brought her palms up to her flushed cheeks. "Oh, Eli." She turned away. The next second, she spun in a full twirl so the strings of her *kapp* framed her face and she clasped his outstretched hands again. "*Jah*. Of course I will marry you, you big oaf." Relief and joy fluttered through her as she threw her arms around him. "It's always been *jah*. Why did it take you so long to get here?"

"You scared me for a moment when you hesitated." His eyes washed over her face and Sarah allowed the love she'd always felt for him to finally emerge unshackled and unrestrained. "I don't deserve you," Eli said, almost as if he thought she might evaporate into the blinding stream of sunlight coming through the dormer.

She grinned. "True, but we'll work on that."

"I love you, Sarah."

She closed her eyes, savoring the sound. "Say it again."

"I love you, Sarah," he whispered. "I love you and I have since the day I first laid eyes on your beautiful face. I'll say it as often as you like and as often as it takes me to convince you."

Her eyes danced and her heart swelled. "You know what the *Englischers* say."

He laughed. "No, what do they say?"

She cocked her head. "Actions speak louder than words."

"I can do action," he murmured, his lips sweeping down to capture hers.

"I'm so happy, Eli. Our cup overflows."

Epilogue

The *boppli's* blue eyes danced with merriment and life as she ran along the banks of the Ohio River. Not far behind, her tall, handsome *dat* chased her. Each time he'd graze his fingers against the back of her lavender dress, he'd deliberately let go and allow her to surge ahead again.

"Come play tag wid us, *mamm*!" Miriam Troyer screamed and then fell into a torrent of toddler giggles.

"Yes, *mamm*, come play 'wid' us." Eli winked at Sarah as she sat on the heavy woolen blanket and unpacked the picnic lunch she'd prepared for her family.

"Not now, Miriam," she laughed. "I've got to get your lunch ready." But even though she argued, she knew she'd be convinced to join in the fun before her current task was completed. Sarah found it hard to refuse either one of them anything.

She and Eli had been married now for over three years and had been blessed with Miriam, not long after their first anniversary. The *boppli* brought so much joy, Sarah's heart overflowed. It seemed the scars on her soul had finally been healed. She now had the happy life and family she'd always wanted.

The only thing that could possibly spoil her *gut* mood was Miriam's constant gloating over her namesake. It had been Eli's idea to name their *dochder* after the older woman. But Sarah had readily agreed. If not for Miriam, they might never have found their way to each other. When Sarah had confronted Miriam about her meeting with Eli, she'd simply winked at her and walked away.

"A penny for your thoughts?" Eli asked, walking up to the blanket with Miriam enfolded in his strong arms. Sarah's heart beamed with pride for her *mann* and her child. It seemed fitting that they now enjoyed the very meadow along the river bank that Levi, Eli and she had played along as *kinner*. Their oak tree was not ten yards away and could provide shade for later if the afternoon sun became too much for little Miriam. Eli had brought his pocketknife so they could carve Miriam's initials alongside theirs after lunch was completed.

"I was just thinking how handsome you look," Sarah admitted, eyes downcast. "Holding our *boppli*. You can't imagine how many times I've fantasized about this very scene playing out in reality every time you held Samuel or Emma."

Sarah still heard from the adult Emma every Christmas and got an update on how the twins fared. They seemed to be thriving in their new home and would be starting school in a short time. *Gott's* path had been clear and everything had worked out according to *His* plan. Of that, Sarah was sure.

"*Denke*," Eli said with a laugh as he sank down onto the blanket.

Miriam immediately grabbed for an apple and tried to bite it. Her tiny teeth wouldn't allow it and she frowned and threw the apple down.

"It's broken, *mamm*."

Eli produced his knife and began cutting it into pieces for her. Miriam had her *vader* wrapped around her tiny fingers.

"You'll spoil her, Eli," Sarah chided but she'd probably do the same. Miriam was the joy of her life. And so was her *vader*.

Eli reclined back on the blanket and took her hand in his. "Did you ever think we'd end up here? So happy. Life is *gut*, Sarah Troyer."

***

Emma loves to hear from all her readers. Since she is retired, you can find her on her author Facebook page, or send her an email at emma@emmaschwartzauthor.com.

The Amish Twins by Emma Schwartz ©2016 All Rights Reserved

This book is a work of fiction. Names, characters, places and incidents are the products of the author's imagination. Any resemblance to actual events, locales or persons, living or dead, is entirely coincidental. No part of this publication may be reproduced, distributed, or transmitted in any form or by any means, including photocopying, recording, or other electronic or mechanical methods, without the prior written permission of the publisher.

Made in United States
North Haven, CT
01 August 2022